THE WILD MAGIC TRILOGY
BOOK 1

Begone the Raggedy Witches

CELINE KIERNAN

CANDLEWICK PRESS

With thanks to all at Pavee Point for their help.

First U.S. paperback edition 2019

Library of Congress Catalog Card Number 2018958177
ISBN 978-0-7636-9996-3 (hardcover)
ISBN 978-1-5362-0874-0 (paperback)

19 20 21 22 23 24 MVP 10 9 8 7 6 5 4 3 2 1

Printed in York, PA, U.S.A.

This book was typeset in Joanna.
The illustrations were done in pen and ink.

Candlewick Press
99 Dover Street
Somerville, Massachusetts 02144

visit us at www.candlewick.com

To Noel, Emmet, and Grace,
always and with all my heart.
And most especially, for Eva, my mam.

The Raggedy Witches

The moon was strange the night the witches came and Aunty died. The colour of brass and huge, it seemed to fill the sky. It stared down at the car as Mam drove in and out of dark country valleys, and blotted the stars with its milky light.

Mup didn't like it. She wanted to tell Mam that. She wanted to start a conversation, but Mam was different tonight too. Like the moon, Mam was strange. Usually they would sing as Mam drove back from the hospital: songs from the radio, songs from their heads. Or they would talk and make up stories and Mam would explain things. (*What are the stars, Mam? They're burning planets, like our sun, only so distant that their light is cold and glittering.*) But tonight the radio was mute and so was Mam, and Mup sat in a tense bubble of silence under the glaring moon, her head buzzing with questions that Mam was not willing to answer.

Mup looked across at her little brother, Tipper. He was fast asleep, his hands curled on his knees, his small mouth open and drooling onto the straps of his car seat. Tipper wasn't much use for conversation, but it would have been nice had he been awake. He could have laughed at the moon, maybe, and—by being so small—he might have made Mup feel big. Gently, Mup reached across and covered Tipper with the car blanket. He went on sleeping, and she rested her head against the window and watched the night flow by.

A car passed, its full beams making Mam curse, and Mup shut her eyes against the glare. For a long time she didn't open them again. She must have fallen asleep without knowing because she was enjoying a lovely dream about warm Swiss roll and custard when the car bumped and she woke up.

Outside, the night was still streaming past. Mup had slumped against the door with her face tilted to the sky, and she was looking up through the branches of the roadside trees. The trees were falling away and falling away as the car sped by, and there were witches in the branches, and they were following the car.

Mup wasn't startled—half asleep as she was,

with the taste of warm custard in her mouth—but she frowned up at the witches with an inkling that something wasn't right. Gradually, the cold of the window stole into her sleepy brain and the thrum of the engine made itself real. All the little squeaks and rattles of a car in motion became solid around her, and as the dream calm slipped away, Mup was filled with the knowledge that she was awake, and there were witches in the trees, following the car.

There were men witches and women witches, and they leapt from branch to branch, racing along at tremendous speed. They were nothing but shadows among shadows, so that Mup had to strain her eyes to see them. She watched for so long that she began to fall asleep again, half convinced she was dreaming after all. Then one of the witches jumped the gap between two trunks, her silhouette dark against the fine grey of the sky. She descended in a falling arc, her clothes blown back like ragged black wings. As her pale hands reached for the branches of the next tree, she looked down into the car and met Mup's eyes.

Mup sat up straight, suddenly afraid.

The witch's face was a pale, bright oval, her black eyes expressionless. She tilted her head in contemplation of the little creature before her, and all the world slowed to the space between heartbeats. For an endless moment, the witch's gaze filled the night, pressing Mup down and down until she felt small and useless and insignificant. Then the witch was gone.

Mup's heart resumed beating. She breathed deep. She jerked forward, craning to see out the window. The witch had passed into the next tree, her clothes fluttering behind her. Travelling hand over hand through the branches, effortlessly pacing the car, she didn't bother to look down again, and neither did her shadowy brothers and sisters.

Mup glanced at Mam, grim-faced and hunched over the steering wheel.

Aunty had said that if Mup ever saw witches, she was to tell. "It doesn't matter what they might want," Aunty had said, holding a hand up to silence Mup's questions. "All you need to know is that if you see one, you are to tell me. But only tell me—you hear? Your mother and father don't need to know."

Mup looked back up into the trees. When Aunty told you to do something, you did it. You did it properly. But Mup had never expected the witches to be so scary. She had always thought Aunty would be here when they arrived.

Was she really not allowed to tell Mam?

All through the journey home, the witches tracked the car, and Mup tracked the witches. Sometimes she'd see them cross the gaps between trees — one, two, three, four, five, six of them — their billowing clothes and pale features sharp against the sky. But mostly they raced through the shadows, hard to see, harder still to believe in.

Abruptly, the trees ended and Mup found herself gazing into empty stars. She knelt up, twisting against her seat belt, and looked behind as the trees diminished in the distance. There was no sign of the witches.

Mam turned the car, and the headlights splashed the front of their house, illuminating the flower beds, the bushes, the big chestnut trees. Mup stayed kneeling, staring out the back window while Mam opened the hall door and returned to take Tipper from his car seat.

"Come on, Mup," Mam said, hefting Tipper's sleeping weight onto her shoulder.

Mup hesitated. A storm had risen, and the garden was alive with sound. The chestnut trees churned like the sea, their leaves tumbling into the fan of light which spilled from the hall door. Mam's hair whipped around her tired face, slipping into her mouth and getting in her eyes.

"Mup!" she cried impatiently.

Mup took a deep breath and dived from the car. The night was a frenzy around her, and she ran as fast as she could across the yielding lawn. *Hurry, Mam,* she thought. *Hurry!* Behind her, Mam slammed the car door and slowly crunched her way up the gravel drive. Over the noise of the storm, through the churning of the trees, came a heavy fluttering sound, like cloth in the wind. Then Mup was in the orange warmth of the hall, and Mam was on her heels slamming the door shut and shaking the storm from her hair.

The house was warm. It was quiet and it was sane. It sealed the horrible night outside.

Mam sighed as she passed up the corridor. "Get your jammies on. I'll make supper in a minute."

"Mam," called Mup, wanting—despite what Aunty had said—to tell her about the witches.

"Shush. Don't wake Tipper." Mam had already turned the corner into Tipper's room, and there was a quiet click from within as she switched his night-light on. Sensible light added itself to the familiar hallway, and Mup fell silent, feeling unsure.

But I did see them, she thought. *I wasn't dreaming . . . was I?*

Badger came nudging out of the kitchen, his big

flat head pushing the door to one side. He grinned his doggy grin, whining with joy, his butt wagging as fast as his tail.

"Hey, boy," whispered Mup. "Hey." Her old friend thumped his tail against the walls and lumbered his head up under Mup's arm, snuffing the interesting journey smells from her hands and coat, licking her face so she had to push his slobbery kisses away. She laughed despite herself. "Did you miss me?"

But already Badger was looking past her at the front door, and the hairs on his neck were stiff under her fingers. A low growl rumbled in his chest.

Mup turned to see. It was just the front door, solid and strong as ever. The two long glass panels on either side reflected Mup and Badger back at themselves: an old black Labrador going grey at the muzzle and a dark-eyed girl dressed in a bright red jacket. Both had anxious expressions, both were watching the door. The wind moaned and rattled the letter box. It battered the sturdy wood and hissed against its fragile glass. Mup hugged her arms protectively around Badger's neck and wondered if Mam had turned the key in the lock.

"You'll never guess," she whispered in Badger's ear, "what I saw in the trees."

The phone rang, and they both leapt, hearts hammering.

It rang again, its shrill call slicing the air.

"Mup!" called Mam. "Answer the phone."

Mup looked back at the front door. The wind was pounding at it now. The dark outside pressed itself against the glass.

"Mup!" called Mam. "The phone!"

Mup edged backwards, her arm around Badger's neck. Without taking her eyes from the thumping door, she picked up the phone. "Hello, Dad," she said.

Dad's laugh came from far away, thin and hissing. "How do you always know it's me?"

Mup shrugged. Outside, the storm paused suddenly, as if listening to the two of them talk. On the phone table beside Mup there was a photo: Dad's dark face smiling under his yellow helmet, his welder held up in greeting. The orange girders of an oil rig surrounded him, the sky and the sea joined together behind him in a cheerful, seamless blue.

Mup closed her eyes and tried to make a path to Dad in her mind. This was a little trick she had with telephones. Usually it was easy: she would just relax and let her thoughts spin down the line, and there the other person would be standing and

8

smiling as if right next to her. But for some reason Mup couldn't bridge the distance between her and Dad tonight.

She frowned. "Is the sun shining where you are, Dad?"

Dad laughed again. "I'm only in Scotland," he said. "We have the same night and day as you."

"Oh, yes," she said. Sometimes the places Dad lived didn't have the same night and day — sometimes Mup lost track. Her eyes slid to the door again. What if she told Dad about the witches? Would that be OK? Probably not. Aunty never said much to Dad about anything.

"I missed you earlier," Dad said. "Were you up with Aunty Boo?"

"Yes."

"Is Aunty . . . ? How is she?"

"She's not the same. Mam is sad."

There was no noise but the echoey silence of the phone. Then a little sound, like a sigh.

"Dad. I think Aunty Boo might go to heaven."

The phone gaped again for a little while, as though Dad had been swallowed into a big hole. Badger flopped at Mup's feet, his fright forgotten. In the kitchen Mam was filling the kettle and shuffling about and sighing. Badger looked up at Mup with big, listening eyes.

Dad's voice hissed up from far away again. "Mup," he said, and then stopped as though he couldn't finish.

"Mam is very tired, Dad." Mup tried to fit everything into that sentence. The way there were no more songs or conversations. How Mam was so far away, how empty the house felt, and how dark the night was, now that Aunty was gone.

"Mupsie," Dad said, his voice humming through cables and lines under the sea, over the land, from him to her, so far, so far. "Your mam loves Aunty Boo so much. She loves her so much. Because . . . because . . ."

"Because Aunty Boo was good to Mam when she was a little girl."

There was a small pause on the line: Dad, far away, deciding what words to use, maybe.

"Yes," he said at last.

"Aunty is like Mam's mam."

"Yes."

"I wouldn't want Mam to die, Dad."

"Well, that's how your mam feels about Aunty Boo."

10

"I don't want Aunty Boo to die, Dad."

"No. I don't either . . . I'd be there if I could, pet. This bloody storm. It won't last much longer. Soon as they can, they'll get a 'copter out and I'll be home. OK?"

Mup nodded into the phone.

"OK? Mup?"

"OK, Dad."

"Can I have Mam?"

"OK, Dad."

"Mup? I love you."

"I love you too, Dad."

Mam took the phone and stood talking quietly in the kitchen. She didn't talk about Aunty Boo; she just asked how Dad was and kept saying, "Let's not talk about that now. Let's not talk about that," very gently over and over, and, "When can you come home . . . ? But when do they think . . . ? Do they think that it will be soon . . . ? I love you too. I wish you were here . . . Yes. Yes. I know."

Mup kept her eyes riveted to the front door as she backed into her bedroom. To her shock, the too-big moon was peering in at her window. Mup did not like the way it stared at her. Badger seemed unperturbed, though, and he trotted straight past

Mup and scuffled around on the rug until he got comfy. Determined to avoid the moonlight, Mup sidled along her bedroom wall until she was close enough to dive into bed. She burrowed deep, so only her eyes showed over the duvet.

I won't sleep until you're gone, she told the watching moon.

The radiator clicked and sang under the window. Badger snored. In the kitchen Mam talked quietly, then fell silent. The house filled with the settlings and sighs of night-time.

The moon moved slowly across Mup's window until it shone straight down onto her bed. Frowning, she withdrew her feet from its milky light. Heavy as sand, the moonlight collected in pearly mounds, thickening and softening and growing warmer until . . . Oh!

Mup lost her wary frown.

It was only Aunty Boo sitting on the end of her bed! As round and solid as any other night when Mup would wake to find her moving about, putting clothes into drawers or quietly picking up toys and tidying shelves of books.

In his sleep, Badger sighed a happy sigh. Aunty was here. Everything was OK.

"Hello, Pearl," said Aunty. She never called Mup anything but Pearl, or Tipper anything but Robert, and she always called Mam Stella, which was Mam's real name. "Why aren't you asleep? It's much too late for children to be awake."

"I got a fright."

"Oh." Aunty sighed. "Well. I'm sorry. I didn't mean to scare you. I just came to settle a few things with your mother before I head off."

"Head off? Head off where?"

Aunty huffed and motioned her hand as if Mup's question was unimportant.

"You going to heaven?" persisted Mup.

Aunty looked mischievously from the corner of her eye and tucked the covers in around Mup's feet. "There now," she said.

All of a sudden, the questions were gone from Mup's head. All she felt was safe and secure; all she felt was sleepy. Aunty hummed her usual quiet lullaby, and—as always—Mup's eyes slipped shut. She floated gently on the song. She was almost entirely asleep before she remembered she had a message for Aunty.

"It wasn't you that gave me a fright, Aunty," Mup murmured. "It was . . ." She searched drowsily for a good name for the creatures that had followed Mam's car. She smiled. "It was the raggedy witches," she said.

Aunty's hand bit down hard on Mup's foot.

"Ow! Aunty! My foot!"

"What did you just say?"

"I said, 'Ow! My foot!'"

Something in Aunty's expression snagged Mup's attention. She sat up. "It wasn't you that gave me a fright," she insisted. "It was the witches."

"What kind of witches?"

Mup made a face. "Creepy ones," she said. "They had pale skin and black eyes. They wore raggedy cloaks."

Aunty's face crumpled as though she had a pain. "Black eyes?" she whispered. "Pale faces? You . . . you saw those kind of witches here, Mup?"

"They were in the trees, following our car."

Aunty was up from the bed at that and over to the window like a woman half her size. "By grace," she muttered, scanning the garden outside. "By grace, I'll be condemned and roasted in a fire before I let that happen!"

Mup flung back the covers and ran to her. "Let *what* happen?" she cried. "You never told me what they do! Are they bad, Aunty? Are they from Mam's mam?"

Mup felt a thrill of fear at mentioning Mam's mam — but Aunty didn't shush her, as she usually would, or tell her to mind her own business. Aunty just continued scanning the trees as though Mup wasn't even there. Her face was all cold white plains and sharp edges, her expression hard and furious and icy. She turned to Mup, and her eyes were fierce ovals filled with black.

Mup screamed in fright and stumbled backwards, falling onto her butt. Badger instantly leapt between them, his lip raised, his teeth showing, and Aunty drew back. It seemed to take her a moment to recognize the person crouched on the floor in front of her, but when she did, she softened. "Mup," she said in apology.

She was just Aunty again, all kindness and concern now, all softness and regret. But Mup had seen her eyes inky black; she had seen the cold, hard face. And here was Badger, gentle, slobbery Badger, hunched between them, his neck hairs bristling, glaring at Aunty with a growl in his chest.

Mup didn't know what to do, so she just sat there, her hand on Badger's collar, staring.

Something landed on the roof. *Bump.* Then came the patter of sure, light footsteps running effortlessly from one side of the roof to the other. Mup leapt to her feet, and the three of them stood, their differences forgotten, their heads cocked to listen, motionlessly watching the ceiling.

The house held its silence against them and gave nothing away.

Then came the unmistakable sound of the back door opening. Then Mam's voice — *Mam's voice* — murmured, *"Come in."*

Then silence.

Mup took a step towards her bedroom door. The hall outside was smoky with shadows. Tipper's room, straight across from hers, was a gaping hole, his moon-mouse night-lamp a useless blob of yellow light that only made the dark more solid. If she stepped out there, into the hallway, into the dark, what then? To her right, far up the hall, would be the treacherous front door. To her left, more doors: Mam's door, the sitting-room door, the playroom, and, at the very end, the kitchen.

The kitchen, where, flanked by Wellington boots and raincoats and dog toys, stood the back door. The back door that led into the moon-watched garden.

The back door which Mam had opened. The back door through which something had just entered their house.

Mam!

Mup ran for the hall. Aunty jerked her back.

"No, Pearl."

"But Mam is on her own with them!"

"I said no!"

Mup fell silent. There was no arguing with Aunty when she had that expression.

"Go back to bed, Pearl," Aunty said, quite gently. "I'll handle this." She walked around the corner and up the hall, her footsteps fading into the gloom.

Mup waited for the sound of the kitchen door opening. She waited for the screaming or shouting or whispering to begin. She waited and nothing happened. Nothing at all. Aunty had disappeared into the corridor as though the air itself had soaked her up.

"Go back to bed." That's what Aunty had told her. "I'll handle this." And Aunty knew best. Aunty always knew best. Mup waited, listening. Still the silence went on.

She looked at her bed, so safe and warm. She looked at the hallway, so empty and dark.

She took a deep breath and stepped out of her bedroom door.

Visitors
for Mam

At the far end of the long, dark hall, a thin sliver of light shone through the partially opened kitchen door. It reflected in Badger's toffee-coloured eyes as he looked up at Mup. "You shouldn't follow me," she whispered. "Go back to bed." But Badger just wagged his tail, as if to say, "I trust you." Mup put her hand on his warm neck, and they walked up the hall together.

"*There's nothing in this house that's going to hurt you, Mup.*" Mam always said that after a scary movie or a bad dream when Mup would be afraid. "*The only thing here is love. Besides, ghosts and monsters are nothing to be afraid of. All the bad things in this world are done by people.*"

But *aren't witches a kind of people?* thought Mup. If so, had Mam really invited them into their house? Mup swallowed hard, then pushed open the door.

The big lights were off, and the kitchen was dimly lit by the low lamps. Mam sat at the table, her hands limply folded, watching the moon through the window. The room was perfectly calm and still, the tock of the cabbage clock over the stove the only noise.

Badger tick-ticked away across the tiles and lay down by the fridge. Mup remained on the threshold, her hand on the door handle, staring. The cold of the floor at Mup's feet told her that she was awake. The creatures standing around Mam made her wish she was asleep.

Badger should be protecting us, thought Mup. *That's his job.* But where was Badger—now that she needed him? Where was he? Lying by the fridge with his chin on his paws, his brown eyes untroubled.

A huge tear brimmed over and slid down Mup's cheek. It trembled beneath her chin for a moment and fell to the floor. "Mam?" she whispered hoarsely.

The six witches that stood around Mam looked up. One was the very tall witch who had stared down at Mup in the car. Mup saw for the first time that she had a long silver streak in her hair. Gently, this witch put her hand on Mam's shoulder, as if she knew Mam, as if they were friends.

"Mam!" cried Mup, horrified at how pale and dead and heavy the witch's hand was, and at how Mam didn't seem to notice it at all. "Mam."

Mam did not look her way.

Mup dashed the tears from her eyes and turned to a patch of moonlight that was lurking by the wall. "Make her answer me, Aunty. Tell her to get up."

The patch of moonlight shifted unhappily. "I can't," it whispered. "I'm not really here."

"You are here!" exclaimed Mup, shocked that Aunty would stand there uselessly instead of fixing things. "I *seen* you, Aunty! We *talked*! You told me to go to bed, you said you'd handle it and now you're doing nothing."

The patch of moonlight shivered and sighed. "I didn't think they'd be so strong here," it whispered. "I'm . . . I'm not what I once was."

Determined to get closer to Mam, Mup began to sidle her way around the edge of the room. The witches watched her. They wore just the faintest of smiles; there was just the faintest, faintest hint of amusement on their faces. As Mup came near, Badger thumped his tail and looked up at her without lifting his head from his paws. She slipped in behind him. His fur warmed her skin. The fridge door was cold through the fabric of her pyjamas. *I really am awake,* she thought.

"Why doesn't he bark at them?" she whispered.

"Because," answered the moonlight, "they've convinced him they belong."

"But they don't belong here, Aunty. You told me that. We're the ones who belong here. *We* are!"

"I used to think so . . ." Aunty's voice was barely there, just a thistledown tickle at the back of Mup's mind. "But look at them. They're so strong. They shouldn't be so strong here. Oh, Pearl, I hadn't realized how dependent things were on my being here. I thought I'd set everything up so your mother would be safe from them even when I was gone. How will she ever survive without me?"

"Without you? Aunty, you said you'd sort the witches out if they came! If you knew you might not be here, why didn't you answer any of my questions about them? Why didn't you show me how to fight them for myself?"

. A sound like static began to fill the room. The tall witch with the silver streak in her hair was whispering wordlessly. Her witch brothers and sisters were whispering too. Their voices chased the questions from Mup's mind. They made it difficult to think.

21

Mup slapped her hands over her ears. "Mam!" she shouted. *"Mam, help!"*

Mam flinched and opened her eyes, turning her head as if to find her daughter.

The tall witch tutted and snaked cold, smooth arms around her. "No need to worry about that," she murmured in Mam's ear. "That's only noise."

Mam's head dropped back and, even though Mup kept yelling, Mam's eyes drifted peacefully shut.

A grip like iron clamped onto Mup's arm, and a sharp voice hissed in her ear. "Hush, Pearl. You'll wake the baby." It was Aunty: still made of moonlight, but full and clear and solid again—raging.

"Aunty. You're back!"

Aunty frowned down at herself. "So I am," she muttered.

It's because you got angry, thought Mup. *You got angry, and it brought you back.*

Aunty glared across at Mam. "Stella!" she snapped. "Those creatures have nothing to do with you. Stop this nonsense and get over here to your child!"

Mup relaxed. This was Aunty's "I mean it" voice. No one ever resisted that voice. Mam would get to her feet now. She would shake free of the witch's grip. She would cross the floor. She would put her arm around

Aunty's waist and her hand on Mup's shoulder, and she would turn with them to face the witches. The three of them would win.

Mup slipped her hand into Aunty's and jutted her chin, waiting.

But Mam did not come.

Instead, the tall witch straightened slowly and Mam straightened with her. The tall witch, her eyes on Aunty, slid her arms around Mam's waist and leaned her pointed chin on Mam's shoulder. She began to sway. The others swayed too. Like strands of seaweed around a corpse, they held Mam at their centre and she, as lifeless as a corpse beneath the water, floated in their arms.

Aunty's eyes narrowed. "Who are you?" she asked the tall witch. "I don't recognize you."

"I am Magda."

Mup thought the witch's voice was like wind rustling through rushes—a low dryness of sound.

"You seem to be the one in charge here, Magda," said Aunty.

"Well, you certainly are not. Not anymore. Else we could never have found the lost heir."

Mup gripped Aunty's hand tight in fear. "They *are* from Mam's mam," she whispered.

Aunty squeezed her hand reassuringly. "My sister must trust you a great deal," she said to the witch.

"I have earned the queen's trust."

"Yes. And I can just imagine what you had to sacrifice in order to gain it. You and your companions were obviously born with a lot of magic. I know my sister. She would never let anything as powerful as you survive, not unless she had absolute control over you."

"Anything I've given the queen I've given gladly."

"I'd say you've given her *everything*—every ounce of loyalty, every scrap of obedience."

"We give our obedience freely, Duchess, and are rewarded for it." The witch's eyes slid to Mam's blank and drifting face. "Can you say the same of your minions?"

"Stella is not my minion! She's free and happy."

The witch almost laughed. "You stole her from her mother."

"I *rescued* her."

"You sealed her away from the Glittering Land."

"I kept her *safe*. I gave her everything she ever wanted!"

The witch sighed as if bored now of the conversation. "You gave her everything but choice, Duchess. Who knows what she might have become had you allowed her to explore her true nature. In any case, your dominion over her is done. Your time has passed. Goodbye." Magda gestured to her companions, and the group of witches began drifting to the door, carrying Mam with them.

Mup cried out "NO!" and dived for Mam.

Aunty jerked her back. "Don't touch her!"

The back door swung open, and pale moonlight spilled in. As the witches guided Mam into the blue rectangle of light, her hair drifted upwards, lifted by an invisible current. Her feet left the ground. Mup knew with absolute certainty, then, that the witches were going to take her mam. They were going to float her away — and if Mup didn't do something to stop them, no one else would.

She shoved free of Aunty and grabbed Mam.

As soon as they touched, the whole of Mup's body came alive with power. It flowed, crackling and electric, from Mam. She was alive with it.

Mam and Mup spun together, alone. Mup saw her mam growing — expanding and expanding, until she was a great, strong, beautiful giant striding across the world. Mup was just a tiny speck on the surface of Mam's power — a power that was dark and wonderful and so very much bigger than them both.

Then Aunty pulled Mup away and there was nothing—just quiet and dark.

Then there were colours.

Mup swam towards the colours and they were Aunty: her fuchsia-pink cardigan, her lime-green T-shirt, her blue, blue eyes. Aunty was shaking her. Her voice was out of focus as if under water, but her fear came through full blast: ". . . don't touch her! I told you! I said don't touch her . . ."

Mup groaned.

Aunty hugged her fiercely. "Don't touch her, Pearl. OK? Don't touch your mam."

"OK, Aunty," Mup said. She was dazed, her voice muffled against Aunty's huge bosoms. "I won't."

"What did you see?" whispered Aunty, sitting Mup upright.

"Mam was . . . Mam was big and strong. She was like . . ." Mup wanted to say, She was like a tidal wave, but at the kitchen door Mam was still drifting helplessly in the witches' arms, and she looked nothing like a tidal wave.

The witches floated out into the garden, guiding Mam across the luminous white of the frosty lawn. Aunty and Mup followed. The sound of the river in the next field seemed to pull the witches forward, reeling them in. Mam, her dark hair drifting upwards, her arms lifted slightly, her toes hovering inches above the ground, allowed them to carry her towards the belt of trees at the end of the garden.

The witches ignored Aunty and Mup. Mam absorbed all of their attention, and they drifted around her, the billowing strips of their clothes, their waving fronds of hair, now obscuring her, now revealing her as they moved into the shadow of the trees.

"They're heading for the border," whispered Aunty. "They're taking her back."

"Is the border here?" gasped Mup. "Next to the house?"

"Over the border" was where Mam had been born. Mup had only ever heard it mentioned in hushed and fearful tones. She was stunned to discover that all this time it had been so close to home.

"I thought I'd brought her up safe and ordinary," moaned Aunty. "I never thought they'd be interested in her."

The outline of the azalea bushes was perfectly visible through her body now. Looking up into her face, Mup could see the night sky, all full of stars. "You're getting invisible again, Aunty."

Aunty nodded, and a tear slipped out and ran down her cheek. "I've lost. They're taking your mother."

"Stop them!" cried Mup. She grabbed at Aunty, but her hand passed right through her. "Get angry, Aunty! Get angry at the witches! Don't let them take Mam to that terrible place!"

Aunty helplessly shook her head. "I'm not in charge here anymore."

Terrified, Mup turned and shouted the first thing she could think of. "Mam! Who'll change Tipper's nappies if you're not here?"

Mam paused. She bobbed about at the heart of the dark cloud of witches, not looking at anything in particular, but Mup thought she might be listening.

"Who'll make our breakfast, Mam?"

Mam's face remained expressionless, her hooded eyes glistening like ink. Behind the hedge, the river roared and gurgled. Mup ran forward, and the witches rose swiftly out of her reach, carrying Mam with them. Mup swiped at the air between them. "I can't reach you, Mam," she cried. "I can't reach."

A small frown appeared between Mam's eyebrows, as if she could just about see Mup — tiny

28

and distant—frantically waving below. But still she drifted upwards. Five feet above the garden she floated. The leaves of the trees were a mottled backdrop to her remote face. Starlight haloed her head.

"Stella." Aunty was nothing but a silver outline now, filled in with the night. "Sweetheart. Please don't go with them."

Mam looked down with her black, black eyes. The witches draped their arms around her, one laid her head on Mam's shoulder. They watched like cats, not even slightly concerned.

"I'm so tired, Aunty," whispered Mam.

"Oh, darling, I know! I've been sick such a long time. And all that long time you've done so much for me. You were wonderful to me, Stella. So wonderful. You were . . ." Aunty searched for the right word. "Stella, you were *great*."

That word: *great*. It meant so much. It came from somewhere deep down in Aunty's heart. It carried every hour Mam had spent by Aunty's side, every long trip to the city hospital, every whisper, every laugh, every genuine moment of love from the last six months and from their entire lifetime together, piled high and passed between them on the frosty air.

Mam's face softened.

"That's all over now, though, Stella," said Aunty. "It's your time now. Time for you to live a little."

Again Mam's eyes drifted to Mup. Mup waved hopefully, but at the sight of her daughter, standing down there on the frosty ground, Mam just seemed tired again — tired and lonely — and she began to turn away.

"Mam!" cried Mup. "Don't leave me!"

Mam paused. She sagged. A fat tear rolled down her cheek, reflecting the stars and the moonlight. Mup realized that it had been a long time since she'd seen her mam cry — not since Aunty Boo had first fell ill, and that was a very long time ago indeed.

"Oh, Mam," she said softly. "I'm sorry you're sad."

That seemed to crack something inside of Mam, and she sobbed, a big, hard, unexpected sob, like a stone heaved up from her chest. She slid a fraction from the witches' arms. Mup stepped forward, reaching, but Aunty pushed her gently aside and took her place. "Stay back, Pearl."

Aunty took a deep breath and lightly grabbed Mam's foot.

The witches didn't fight. Mam just slithered through their grasp, and they let her go with nothing more than a curious tilt of their heads. Mam folded gently into Aunty's arms, and together she and Aunty sank to their knees on the moonlit grass, where Mam wept and wept, and Aunty cradled her.

"Oh, she can't leave," said the tall witch with mild surprise. "How completely useless of her."

"Yes, Magda," hissed Aunty. "You go back and tell the queen that. Tell her there's nothing here for her to fear. Stella will never go back across the border."

The witches were blending with the tree shadows now, drifting backwards on the sound of the river. "You can't make that promise, Duchess. Only the heir herself gets to choose that."

Aunty's arms tightened harder around Mam. "She chooses to stay here!" she shouted. "Tell the queen that! Her daughter chooses to stay here!"

"Yes!" cried Mup. "My mam's staying here!"

Magda gave one more half-smile and turned away. The silver streak in her hair was the last thing visible in the darkness, then even that was gone.

Something nudged Mup in the back, and her knees nearly buckled from the fright. But her hands were immediately warm as a great black head lumbered up under her arm and a warm wet nose snuffled her neck. She threaded her arms around Badger's deep chest and buried her face in his doggy-scented fur.

The witches were gone. That was certain. There was no taint or tincture of them to the night, no trace of them in light or shadow. Still Mup scanned the darkness, not ready yet to trust it.

Cradled in Aunty's arms, her face wet with tears, Mam was also staring into the trees.

"They're not offering you anything, Stella," said Aunty. "Believe me. It's a trap. Anyway, your life is here." Aunty closed her hand on Mam's wrist. "Your responsibilities are here."

Aunty and Mam looked across to Mup. Mup didn't like the way Mam's body slumped at the sight of her, the way she sighed and hung her head before getting to her feet. But then Mam held out a hand, and Mup ran to her, and she was in Mam's arms, her arms clenched around Mam's waist, her face buried in Mam's sweater.

Back in the house, Mam lit the range, and they sat by the warm glow of it, Aunty in her big old rocker, Mam on the stool, Mup on the footstool by Aunty's feet.

"What's the queen like?" asked Mam.

"I've told you before," said Aunty. "Your mother is cold, broken, dangerous. She'll destroy you."

Mup nodded earnestly—this was something

they all knew. Aunty had told them: Mam's mam was bad. Mam's mam was dangerous. She must never be spoken of. But Aunty had also told them that as long as everyone behaved, the queen would leave them alone. Hesitantly, Mup chanced a new question (after all, on so strange a night wasn't it possible any question might be answered?): "Aunty, why . . . why did the queen send witches for Mam?"

Aunty sighed. She glanced at Mam. "To see what you are like, maybe? Now that I'm gone and you're next in line to the throne. To see if you're a threat?"

Mup looked at her mam's tired face. A threat? Could Mam—vague, dreamy, distant, and a little disorganized—ever be considered a threat?

"Perhaps she hopes I'd be an asset," said Mam quietly.

There was a long silence. "Your mother would never consider you an asset, Stella. Don't fool yourself of that. You made the right choice staying here. You and the babies are safe now."

The phone rang sharply, and the two women glanced at it.

"Let it ring," said Aunty. "It's not like we don't know who it is."

The phone rang. It rang. It rang. Mup closed her

eyes. This time it was easy to bridge the gap to the other end of the line—in her mind she saw a doctor in the big white corridor of the hospital in the city. He was the nice man who had been taking care of Aunty. His slim brown face was sad. On the tenth ring, he put the receiver down with a shake of his head.

In the quiet that followed, Mup looked up. Mam's eyes were filled with tears.

"So," she said to Aunty, "you're gone."

Aunty nodded. "I'm gone."

"Will you not be coming back?" asked Mup. Was that possible? Life without Aunty? It didn't feel real.

"I'm going to be so lonely, Aunty," said Mam.

"Sure haven't I made you this lovely home?"

"I've no friends. I've no sisters. I'm all on my own."

"Not quite." Aunty gently pushed Mup's shoulder. "Go give your mam a hug, Pearl."

Mup went and wrapped her arms around Mam and held tight. Mam loosely closed her arms about her.

"Well," said Aunty, softly. "Guess I'd better go."

She kissed the top of Mup's head. She placed the palm of her hand on Mam's cheek. Outside, the sun rose above the trees and painted the kitchen with the finest lemon light. It seemed to wash Aunty from the air.

Mup pressed her face in against Mam. The quietness of the house closed in. It was a strange, heavy kind of quiet. Uncomfortable. Was this what the world felt like without Aunty? Mup could feel Mam moving her head left and right, then left again, as if she was looking all around the room. Perhaps she was looking at the empty chair and the empty table, and Aunty's empty slippers by the stove.

Aunty was gone. She was gone.

Mup clenched her arms tighter. "You still have us, Mam," she whispered. "Me and Tipper and Dad."

Mam did not reply, and at last Mup looked up.

"Oh," she said, startled. "What's happened to the light?"

Everything seemed brittle and over-bright. The cups, the table, the stove, the fridge—all of it glittered, strangely flat. Even Badger, asleep in his spot by the fridge, seemed not to breathe.

Mam stood up from Mup's arms. She went to peer down the hall.

Mup ran to her, and slowly they began to walk from room to silent room.

The Decidedly Fragile World

"Is he breathing?" asked Mup, peering between the bars into Tipper's cot.

"Yes," said Mam. "Don't wake him."

"Tipper will miss Aunty, won't he, Mam?"

Mam didn't answer. She frowned out into the garden as she cracked the curtains, causing a spear of sunshine to shaft across the room. It illuminated the circus mobile which Aunty had hung over Tipper's cot. The paper figures were heavy as glass on their cobwebby strings—all the monkeys and elephants and tigers, motionless. Mup touched a finger to the ringmaster's painted leg. He glittered and spun and came immediately to rest.

"Everything feels . . ." Mup searched for the word.

"Fragile," said Mam. "Ready to break."

The two of them jumped as a blast of static shattered the stillness.

"The witches!" cried Mup.

Mam shook her head. "It's not them," she said. "Don't wake your brother."

Tipper was peaceful as a pillow in his cot, his chubby hands thrown up on either side of his round face, his eyelids lightly closed. The blaring noise didn't seem to bother him at all.

"Watch him," said Mam, moving out into the hall. Mup watched him for as long as it took to back to the door, then she followed her mother to the kitchen, where the noise seemed to originate.

It was the TV. It had somehow switched itself on. Mam was standing in the doorway, gazing at it, and as Mup came up behind her, the screen flicked all by itself from one empty channel to another before settling on the news. It showed a helicopter leaning drunkenly in a field, dazed men in jumpsuits being helped from the door. Mam strode across and turned up the sound.

". . . four hours after the helicopter from the North Sea oil rig went missing, search-and-rescue were amazed to discover it in this field in Cornwall. The crew and passengers are said to be disoriented but unharmed. Concern has been expressed, however, for crew member Daniel Taylor, who—despite having been named on the flight list—is nowhere to be found. Concerns that Mr. Taylor may have fallen from the craft are being discounted as 'unlikely.' However, the crew seems to have little knowledge of the circumstances of his disappearance, nor of how they managed to be blown so radically off course."

"Daniel Taylor," said Mup quietly. "That's Dad."

Mam pressed the TV to mute.

"Mam," insisted Mup. "They're talking about Dad!"

Instead of answering, Mam flung open the back door, where she stood in a flood of frosty sunshine, staring down to the shadow-drenched trees that hemmed the garden. Mup moved to her side. There was a cat in the shelter of the trees. It dipped its chin when it saw Mup's mother, and tilted its head as if in greeting to her. Mup did not feel at all surprised when it spoke.

"Highness," it said. "Will you cross?"

Mam's fingers closed tight against the wood of the door frame. "Has the queen taken my husband?"

The cat wagged its head, maybe yes, maybe no. "There are any amount of folk interested in tempting the heir back over the border, now your aunt is not around to stop us. Who knows which of them might have taken your man, hoping to draw you across."

"That's my dad you're talking about!" cried Mup. "Give him back!"

The cat huffed. It lifted its luminous eyes to Mam. "Will you rescue him? After all, who else will, if you do not? A spawn of earth lost in the Glittering Land — who else would bother to care? You do recall how to cross, don't you, Highness? The duchess hasn't so addled your instincts that you can't recall your way home."

"This is her home!" cried Mup.

The cat tutted and rose to its feet, turning away as if to go.

Mup ran forward. "Bring back my dad!"

"You needn't have stolen him," shouted Mam from the doorway. "Why didn't you just ask me to come home? Why did you assume you had to take?"

The cat's eyes slid to where Mup stood angrily between them. "Why indeed?" it said, and with a final sneer, it walked away into the shadows. In the unnatural stillness of the morning, the sound of the river beyond the trees was very loud. The cat seemed to disappear into it.

Mam stormed back into the kitchen and began taking things from cupboards — baby bottles, nappies, wipes. "Get your boots," she told Mup grimly. "Get your coat. Wrap up warm."

"Are we going to cross the border?"

Mam paused, then recommenced throwing things into Tipper's baby bag. "Yes," she said.

"To rescue Dad?"

"Yes."

Heart racing, Mup ran to tell Aunty what they were planning. It was only when she opened the door, and Aunty's bedroom greeted her with all its quietness, that she remembered.

The sun glowed through the yellow curtains and lay on the neat bed, and it seemed unlikely that Aunty, all moonlight now and strangeness, would be there. Still Mup whispered, "Aunty? We're crossing the border. We're going to rescue Dad."

The room seemed to have nothing to say about that, though Mup listened very hard, hoping.

After a moment she gently closed the door. "Well," she said, borrowing Aunty's favourite phrase, "we'll just have to manage as we are."

She decided it was probably best not to go on a rescue mission dressed only in her pyjamas, and so she hurried to her room and flung open her wardrobe. She pulled on her warmest tights — the stripy ones that looked like rainbows. She pulled on her fluffy purple socks and she pulled on her favourite Wellingtons—not the sensible, grown-up black ones, but the old lime-green ones, the ones with the faces like frogs.

There was something about the witches—their cold, dark eyes, maybe, their fluttering black clothes—that made Mup want colours. Not just colours but *colours*: COLOURS! She put on her scarlet wool dress and over the top of that her pink tutu with the skirt made of tulle. The tutu was a little tight over her scarlet dress, but it was covered in spangles and when Mup turned in front of the mirror, she sent rays of light shooting out into the sluggish air.

Good, she thought.

Mam was in Tipper's room, changing Tipper's nappy and getting him ready. Mup could hear that he was not quite awake. She ran past his room, pulling on her red jacket. In the kitchen she rummaged out her favourite hat—the orange one with a rabbit's face and ears on it. She jammed it over her unruly cloud of black hair and took Badger's lead down from its hook. She chose the new lead that Dad had bought Badger for Christmas. It was blue with little yellow bones on it. (*Colours*, she thought. *Colours!*)

It took a long while to wake Badger. He just didn't seem to want to. But eventually she got him to his feet. By the time Mam had finished with Tipper and came into the kitchen, Mup was standing by the back door, with Badger on his lead, a school bag on her back (sandwiches, a flask of orange juice, a packet of cheese-and-onion crisps, and two green apples), ready to go.

Tipper was in his carrier on Mam's back, and he looked at Mup sideways from around the bottle he was sleepily sucking down. There wasn't much of him to see between the thick hat he wore, his bottle, and the side of Mam's head, but he waved a cheerfully mittened hand, and Mup solemnly waved back.

Mam was dressed in jeans and a sensible raincoat, hiking boots, and a cream-coloured hat. She came to a halt in the kitchen doorway, apparently startled at the sight of her daughter's clothes. Mup felt unsure suddenly. Aunty had never liked it when clothes stood out too much. Maybe this outfit was one of those she'd have frowned at?

Mup smoothed her tutu. "Am I too sparkly?" she asked Mam.

Mam seemed to swallow something down into

her chest. She adjusted the heavy baby bag on her shoulder. "You can never be too sparkly, Mup."

Mup nodded.

Mam opened the door and sunshine lit the room. "Let's go rescue Dad."

"Aren't we taking the car?"

"No."

"How will we get there?"

Mam just kept walking through the brittle sunshine, heading for the shadowy trees at the end of the back garden. She took Mup's hand. This was a surprise. Mup tried not to "hang off" her or be "too hot"—things that usually made Mam let go—and they held hands all the way across the lawn and into the shade.

Aunty had never allowed Mup in under these trees. The air had a thick, syrupy feeling to it here, as if the world were asleep and she were walking through its dream. At first, spears of light hit off her dress and made the surrounding trunks sparkle. But soon the trees grew denser and the sparkles stopped. Badger, reluctant at the end of his lead, looked longingly back the way they'd come. There were only golden fragments of garden visible now through the crowding branches. The scent of pine was sharp, the sound of the river much louder than Mup had ever heard.

They broke suddenly into sunshine, and the air roared with the noise of the river.

Mup shaded her eyes against the water-dazzle; she could barely see the other side.

I never knew the stream was that wide, she thought.

"Is this the border?" she shouted.

"Yes," Mam yelled back. "I remember it from when I was little."

"I always thought the border was far away?"

Mup could hardly hear Mam when she muttered, "The border's never far away. No matter where you run, it's always just around the corner."

"What do you think you're *doing?*" cried a familiar voice, and they turned to see Aunty rippling like sun-dapple within the darkness of the trees. Mup cried out in delight, but Mam clamped down on her hand, stopping her from running forward.

"Aunty," said Mam softly. "You should have passed over by now. You know it's not good to hang around."

The sparkly Aunty-shape flung out its arms in exasperation. "But what choice do I have? I'm only gone for one second and you're already running back to your mother!"

"I'm crossing over to rescue Daniel!"

"You're walking right into her arms! You'll end up locked in a dungeon, dead in a gibbet, or worse!"

"Well, what do you want me to do? Leave Daniel to the same fate?"

Aunty shrugged. "You could always find another husband," she suggested weakly.

"Aunty," gasped Mup. "Why would you say that? You like my dad!"

Mam growled. "You should be ashamed, old lady. I thought you crossed the border to get away from that kind of callous behaviour."

"Well, you can't take those babies with you."

"I'm not a baby," said Mup. Aunty gave her a sharp look, and Mup squared her shoulders. "I'm not," she said, straightening her rabbit-eared hat.

"Me the baby!" yelled Tipper, bopping Mam on the head with his bottle. "Me the baby!"

Mam lifted her hand to deflect the bottle's blows, her eyes fixed on Aunty. "I won't abandon Daniel," she said. She turned back to the river, but she looked a little uncertain now, all laden down with bags and baby, her face light-splashed and glittery, staring across to the unseen far bank. Mup grabbed her hand supportively. Mam looked down at her in surprise.

"I'm not what I used to be!" warned Aunty. "If you go over there, I won't be able to help you!"

"Well," said Mam softly, gazing into Mup's eyes, "I'll just have to make do with what I've got, then. Are you ready, Mup?"

Mup nodded.

Mam tugged the straps of Tipper's carrier, tightened her grip on Mup's hand, and together they stepped onto the gurgling surface of the water.

Look how the water ripples around my toes! thought Mup as they took one step then another out into the dancing light. *It's a good thing I wore my Wellingtons.*

"Fishy!" cried Tipper from somewhere high above. "Fishyfish! Fishy!"

Mam quickened her step. "Think floaty thoughts!" she called, raising her voice above the river's roar. "Think purposeful! Think crossing thoughts!"

Crossing thoughts, thought Mup. *Purposeful . . . What does "purposeful" mean?*

Behind her, Badger was slipping and sliding about. He seemed not to know what was expected of him on the river's tumbling surface. Mup tugged his lead. "Think floaty thoughts, Badger!" she yelled. "Think purposeful!"

Badger yowled and spun like a leaf on the end of his lead. Then his feet broke through the surface of the water, and — first knee-deep, then shoulder-deep — he began swimming, a horrified, chin-lifted doggy-paddle in the blinding chaos of light.

"Leave him behind!" yelled Mam.

As if in panic at the suggestion, Badger yowled again and tried to doggy-paddle over to Mup, but he was sinking fast. Soon only his eyes and his desperately upturned snout were visible above the surface.

"Leave him behind, Mup!" yelled Mam again. She was nothing now but a voice and a hand leading to an arm that was swallowed by water-dazzle. "He'll drag us down!"

"I can't leave Badger!"

Badger went under, sucked from sight as quick as a blink. Mup — still clinging to his lead — was pulled down with his weight. The water gave way with a plooping sound, and next she knew she had broken through its rushing surface and plunged after her dog.

How different it was under water. How green and still and cool when compared to the turmoil above. Badger was frantically paddling below her, his eyes upturned to hers. The bright blue lead with all its cheerful little bones stretched between them, preventing him from being whipped away by the current. He doggy-paddled in a wide circle and barked a bright stream of bubbles.

I have you, Badger! thought Mup. *I have you. I won't let you go!*

Overhead, Mam's hand fiercely held her by the wrist. Mup could see the thick crimped soles of Mam's hiking boots puncturing the surface with every step. She could see Mam's wavery outline where she was hunched over, trying to keep hold of Mup and stay above the water at the same time. Mup was certain that up there in the sunshine Mam was still yelling at her to let go of Badger.

Suddenly the water split and Mup plunged even lower as her mam dropped, waist-deep, into the gloom. Mup briefly saw Mam's face, goggle-eyed and frantic, all surrounded in bubbles, then Mam managed to pull her head above the water, and all that could be seen were her bicycling legs, the bottom of Tipper's little boots paddling the surface of the water, and Mam's arm stretched down, clinging furiously to Mup's wrist.

A bubble-bark sounded below, and Mup looked down to see that Badger had reached the pleasantly weedy floor of the river. He was barking up at her as if to say, *Where to, Mup?*

Keep going, Mup thought. *We need to cross the border! We need to get to the other side!*

As though he'd heard her, Badger scrambled forward across the river floor, sending up glittering mud clouds and showers of bright green weed.

Mup began swimming, dragging Mam above like an obstinately struggling balloon.

Soon Mup's boots touched rocks and she too was running across the riverbed, with Badger by her side. *It's a slope!* she thought. *Like a hill under water! I'm running uphill under water!*

A host of little fishes paused to watch her pass.

A hare! they cried, in startled silver voices.

It's just a hat! thought Mup rushing by. *I'm actually a girl.*

But the fish darted away singing, *The hare, the hare, the stitcher of worlds, hippiting, hoppiting, sometimes a girl!*

Mam and Tipper were mostly under water now, but they couldn't seem to get the hang of sinking properly, and they thrashed overhead, caught between the upside world and the down below in a foam of kicking legs and desperately waving arms.

Oh no! thought Mup. *They're drowning!*

"THIS WAY!" Aunty's voice called from the growing brightness ahead. "THIS WAY!"

Mup thought she saw a figure waving from the dazzling light that was coming through the shallower water there. *I mustn't let go,* she thought, struggling forward. *I mustn't let go.* But Badger was pulling at the end of his lead, and the riverbed was slipping and slithering beneath her feet, and Mam and Tipper shouted and tugged at the end of her arm, and everything was swirling and too bright and turning head over head over head over heels until Mup had no choice but to close her eyes.

A Tongue-Tied Crow

I didn't let go, thought Mup.

Nevertheless, when she awoke she was all alone and the world had changed. She leapt up, scattering the autumn leaves which had covered her. She was standing at the top of a small hill. It was covered in graceful trees, and at its base gurgled a bright and shallow stream. Across the stream were more trees—slender and airy, like the ones which surrounded her. They shed gold and copper leaves in luminous drifts, adding to the multitudes that already patchworked the ground.

There was a building visible within the woods across the stream. Mup tilted her head, regarding it closely. If she squinted one eye and closed the other, the building almost looked like her house. Though someone had added a platform to it, and a signal booth, and . . . my goodness, was it a train station?

Mup shaded her eyes to see. *Yes,* she thought. *It is. Someone has turned my house into a train station. What use can a train station be, though, when the tracks have been rolled up like liquorice?* There really was no other way to describe it. Someone had taken the train tracks nearest Mup's house and, working their way out into the countryside for about half a mile, rolled them back along themselves like some spectacularly large coil of wire.

There was no way any train would ever get to that station.

Mup shivered. *I don't like this,* she thought. *What's become of my home? Where's my mam? Where's Tipper?*

A person coughed behind her and a young — if hoarse — voice said:

"*Doesn't matter where your aim,*

No point waiting for a train . . . eh . . . here."

Mup turned to find a raven watching her from the lowest branches of the nearest tree. He was quite a young raven, very black and glossy, and he watched her first from one eye, then the other, waiting for her to reply.

"Um . . ." she said, glancing around to be sure no one else could have spoken. "Um . . . pardon?"

The raven hopped and fluttered. It sighed. Then, as if trying very hard to get every word correct, it said:

"Though the trains here used to run,

The queen has cancelled every one!"

He seemed very pleased with this, and he hopped again and preened his feathers. "That definitely rhymed," he muttered. Then he glanced at Mup in alarm and said, "Fine! It rhymed, just fine. Fined! It rhymed just find!" He trailed off, apparently deflated.

"Have . . . have you seen my mam?" asked Mup. "A lady, with a baby in a . . . in a kind of bag. She might be with . . ." She trailed off, not sure how to explain Aunty's ghost.

"I've seen no baby in a bag,

Not even carried by a hag."

"Lady, I said! Not hag!"

The raven shook his feathers, flustered.

"Can't think of a word to rhyme with Lady . . .

Shady . . . ? Fadey . . . ? Spadey . . . ? Jadey . . . ?"

"Does everything you say need to rhyme?"

The raven sighed.

"Each and every single time."

53

"But why? Doesn't it make it hard to talk?"

The raven jiggled and puffed up his feathers in frustration.

"You know quite well that it is law,

Rhyme's the way we're meant to . . . meant to . . ."

"Caw?" suggested Mup.

The raven glared at her.

"By the feathers on my beak," he said,

"It's the only way that we can speak."

"You seem to find it very hard," observed Mup with sympathy.

The raven sadly agreed:

"That is true.

All my rhyming sounds like . . ."

"Poo?" suggested Mup.

The raven fluffed and sputtered.

"Don't be mad!" cried Mup. "I'm trying to make you not so sad!"

"Rhyming's just a joke for you,

For me it's hard and feels like —"

"Poo?" whispered Mup again — her brain apparently quite stuck on the word.

The raven cawed angrily and fluttered into the air.

"Easy to mock and bully and tease

When you can speak just how you please!"

He flew off into the trees, cawing angrily at the top of his voice.

"I was only trying to help!" called Mup.

She watched him go, thinking what a bad-tempered bird he'd turned out to be, and how glad she was to see the back of him. Then she realized that she was all alone in a strange wood (in a strange world) and she regretted him leaving. She pulled her coat tightly around her and regarded the leaves pattering down and the little stream at the foot of the hill and the strange little train station.

Is that really my house? she thought.

Should she venture down to it? What if there was a different kind of Mup in there, with a different kind of Mam and a strange sort of brother? She wondered if she made her way down there and knocked, who would come to the door?

Maybe, she thought, *the trains don't run because whoever lives there is very, very scary . . .*

A snuffling, scuffling, crashing sound startled her, and she crouched down as something large and dark approached through the bushes to her right. Bright clusters of berries shook, leaves poured down, and Badger came shoving through the slender branches, a very worried look on his face.

Mup leapt for him and hugged his neck. "Badger!" she yelled. "You're safe! I was so worried you'd drowned."

Badger seemed delighted to see her, but he didn't waste too much time licking her face before he turned and pushed back through the shivering berry bushes. He was obviously in a great hurry.

Mup adjusted her backpack, straightened her hat, and followed him deeper into the golden woods. She felt very relieved to find that he was heading in the opposite direction to the strange little house that bore so much resemblance to her own. Soon they reached the top of a leaf-blanketed hill, at the base of which Mam and Aunty were standing over Tipper's tumbled baby-carrier, arguing.

Aunty was all transparent, the brightly coloured leaves and tree trunks showing through her angry face. "It's not right!" she cried. "You can't allow him to stay like that!"

Mam was taking things out of the baby bag and flinging them on the ground. "Why not?" she said. "It's certainly far less for me to carry." She dumped a pile of nappies and threw the bottles on top. "There," she said, slinging the bag back onto her shoulders. "So much lighter. Anyway, it's much safer for him."

"Safer?" cried Aunty. "He's a *dog!*"

Mup was about to speak when something huge and warm and smelling faintly of baby powder burst from a bush and started licking her face. "Augh!" cried Mup. And "Whuuu!" as she and a strong-bodied, fat-pawed, yellow-furred dog rolled downhill to land at Mam's feet.

"Look!" yelled the dog, leaping off Mup and running round and round in an excited circle. "Look! I has a tail!"

Mup sat up in a tumble of leaves, gaping.

"And listen! Listen to this!" The dog sat proudly back on his haunches, cleared his throat, and howled a long and mournful howl.

Badger, who had followed with dignified composure down the hill, winced.

"Tipper," said Mam to the howling dog. "Shush."

"T-Tipper?" asked Mup, astounded.

"Well, of course," tutted Aunty. "Who else would it be?"

The dog wagged his tail. "Guess what, Mup?" He leaned conspiratorially close, managing to drool in Mup's hair as he whispered not so quietly, "I made wee-wee in the bushes!"

Mup scratched her brother tentatively behind his

ear. She wasn't sure which was the more surprising, the fact that Tipper was now a dog, or the fact that he could speak far better than he'd used to as a boy. "Can Badger talk too?" she asked.

"Don't be silly, Mup," said Mam. "Badger is just an ordinary dog."

Mup looked from her brother to her pet and back again. They both cocked their heads at her and lolled their tongues. She couldn't say she saw much difference between them.

Aunty turned on Mam again. "Why are you being so stubborn about this?" she snapped. "I'm telling you, you cannot leave the child like that!"

To Mup's amazement, Mam just shrugged and shoved the baby-carrier under a bush with all the stuff she'd taken out of her bag. "He seems happy enough," she said, regarding her son as he writhed delightedly in the leaves. "Besides, you weren't the one carrying him."

"Oh, of course!" cawed a familiar voice.

"Drop the child! Make him walk!

Tie his tongue so he can't talk!"

They looked up to see the young raven glaring at them.

"Bird!" barked Tipper. "Bird! Bird!"

58

Mam reached down and gently held his mouth closed. "Quiet, Tipper. No one can know we're here."

"*Typical!*" cawed the raven.

"*Better learn your poems, pup,*

It'll be the only way you can . . . the only way you can . . ."

"Speak up," whispered Mup. But she didn't make the mistake of finishing the raven's rhyme for him this time. Failing to manage the task for himself, the angry young bird cawed in frustration and flapped away into the trees, leaving one lonely feather to spiral down in his wake.

"Who in grace was that?" said Aunty.

"Whoever it is," growled Mam, "we need to catch him before he caws our location to the whole of Witches Borough. Come on."

Mup stooped to pick up the raven feather.

"Mup!" cried Mam. "Come on!" And, as Mup watched in open-mouthed amazement, Mam scaled the trunk of the nearest tree and began a rapid, graceful, deadly chase from branch to slender branch, following the raven's voice deep into the woods.

A Captive Crow

"Stella!" yelled Aunty. "Come back here this minute and behave yourself."

But Mam had already disappeared into the treetops.

"Damn it," said Aunty, and she shot up into the branches after her, an angry ball of light, leaving Mup and Tipper and Badger to gape from the ground below. Soon the only thing to be seen of Mam or Aunty were the leaves, which fell in a bright shower of colour as Mam moved from tree to tree.

Tipper prowled an anxious circle. "Oh, Mup," he whimpered. "What we do?"

Badger bounded to the edge of the clearing, woofing and eager.

Tipper scampered over to him, yapping with excitement. "Yes!" he woofed. "Me and Badger chase them! Chase! Chase!"

"What about me?" cried Mup. "There's no way I can keep up with your four legs."

"Climb!" woofed Tipper.

"I . . . I'm not allowed to climb. Aunty said—"

"Mammy climbed!" he said. "Aunty climbed! You climb, Mup!"

The raven's cawing was getting further away now, and Mam was out of sight entirely. Badger backed into the bushes, whining as if to say, "Hurry now, hurry!"

Mup placed her hand on the trunk of the nearest tree. Something seemed to overtake her then, some wonderful, smooth understanding of her mind and body, and suddenly she was slipping upwards through the branches. The leaves were a delightful tickle at her cheeks, the white bark thin and papery beneath her hands as, lithe as a squirrel and just as weightless, she climbed the welcoming tree.

"Wow!" Tipper barked up at her. "Wow!"

Then he was chasing through the leaves below as Mup was racing through the leaves above, the branches springing gladly beneath her hands and feet, for all the world as if this were the only way she'd ever travelled. Tipper and Badger were dashes of black and gold beneath. Her mother was a compass point ahead. Mup followed unerringly in her wake as if following a clearly marked path.

It was exhilarating. It was amazing.

How fast and fluid she was. How graceful. How high above the world.

Mup quite forgot they were chasing another creature until she came to the place where the raven flew above the treetops. Then she heard his terrified caws, and saw his terrified face, and witnessed the puff of loosened feathers as her mother leapt from the branches like a cat and snatched him from the air.

Mup cautiously descended from the treetops. She was not cautious from fear of falling—she'd never felt more secure. She was cautious of this fierce, new version of her mother whom she could see on the ground below pacing to and fro within the tiny space of a forest clearing. Aunty was watching from the shadow of a tree, dappled and uncertain.

"Oh," said Mam. "Oh. The *power*. How could you have taken me from this place? How could you?"

"It was for your own good," said Aunty.

"You've never let me even try to climb trees. You said I was too clumsy! You said I'd fall."

"Maybe you would have."

Mam pointed back the way she'd come. "As soon as I touched that tree, I knew I could climb it. It's like I was *made* to climb it. How could you have kept that from me?"

"Well, what did you expect me to do? I had to keep you safe. Can you imagine people's reaction out in the mundane world if you suddenly started"—Aunty waved a hand to the treetops—"*misbehaving* like that. You'd never have had a chance of fitting in."

Mam clutched her head and made a frustrated sound. "All these years," she said. "All these years of feeling awkward and anxious and—*gah*! I could have been that! I could have felt like *that*!"

Mup finished climbing slowly downwards, her eyes on Mam. She reached the ground and her feet met the soft carpet of leaves, but she did not lift her hands from the trunk of the tree. She was afraid that if she let go she'd go back to being Mup again, just Mup. No longer this bigger, better creature—graceful and sure and part of the forest—no longer part of something larger than herself.

She pressed her hands to the trunk and gazed up into the tree. *Thank you*, she thought.

Above her, the branches swayed in the breeze. *My pleasure*, they seemed to say.

Mup reluctantly let go.

The colours of the forest dimmed a little, as though the trees had stepped away. Mup felt immediately cold and small. She noticed for the first time that Mam had the raven clutched in her hands. The poor thing was too terrified to even struggle.

"Mam," said Mup. "The raven."

Her mother looked down at the stricken bundle of feathers, as if only just remembering it. "Who are you?" she hissed, drawing him close. "Do you know where my husband is?"

The raven shut his eyes as though to cut out the pale and angry face of the woman who held him so tight.

"Mam," said Mup. "You're hurting him!"

"Go easy on him, Stella," said Aunty. "Can't you see he's very young?"

"But who is he?" asked Mam, brandishing the raven at her. "Who is he? And why is he spying on us?"

"I'm only Crow," whispered the raven.

"Don't hurt me so."

"Don't hurt you? I'll wring your neck if you don't tell me where Daniel is."

"Stella!" cried Aunty. "Control yourself!" She was angry now, and—as before—her anger seemed to make her more solid. She snatched the raven from Mam's hands.

"Control myself? I don't even know myself!"

"Oh, tosh!" Aunty snapped, and she strode from Mam to the other side of the clearing, where she snagged a thread of scarlet wool from Mup's dress. She blew on the wool, and, to Mup's amazement, it squirmed to life, lengthening and growing in Aunty's transparent hand.

"Get me a rock, Pearl," said Aunty.

Mup ran and found a rock about the size of her fist. She offered it to Aunty.

"Net!" commanded Aunty. With extraordinary speed, the wool squirmed across to Mup's palm, tickling her as it wriggled in and under and over itself, weaving an intricate net around the stone.

"Oh, Aunty," gasped Mup, touching a finger to the lovely crochet-work which now encased the heavy rock. "Am I able to do that?" (How much better those awful school-time knitting classes would have been, had Mup been capable of commanding the wool like that!)

"Who knows what you can do," snapped Mam. "It's not like *she* was ever planning to tell us." And then to Aunty she said, "I thought you said you'd be no use over here, old lady? I thought you said you'd have no powers."

"You'll need a damn sight more than simple knot magic," muttered Aunty, "if you're to face your mother."

"You just didn't want to help me cross the border."

"That's right," snapped Aunty. "I didn't!" Then to the wool she said, "Bind!" The free end wrapped itself, as quick as you like, into the most complex of knots around the raven's scaly leg.

Aunty released him, and he immediately tried to fly away, jerking the rock from Mup's hand. The weight of the stone pulled him down, crashing him hard to the forest floor. He leapt in panic for the air again, and once again crashed violently to the earth.

"Aunty," cried Mup. "Let him go! He'll hurt himself!"

But Aunty was already crossing to Mam, who still

prowled like a caged tiger within the confines of the small clearing.

"I remember all this," said Mam. "All these beautiful colours. This powerful feeling. I remember it clearly."

"You can't possibly remember. You were only five when we left."

"You told me this was a terrible place. You told me it was bad for me."

"It *is* a terrible place. Your mother *made* it terrible."

"How could you have done this to me? Making me live all those years in that grey world. Making me pretend to be something I wasn't."

Grey world? thought Mup. Surely Mam didn't mean their home? Mup went to object. But then she remembered how small she'd felt after climbing down from the trees, and how colourless—and she closed her mouth, because she realized that she understood exactly what Mam meant.

"But we have a great life there!" cried Aunty to Mam. "We're happy there!"

"I'm not happy! I'm only ever pretending! I only ever feel like I'm playing a part!"

"Oh, everyone feels like that," huffed Aunty. "No matter where they are."

Mam flung up a hand, and power sparked like small lightning between her fingers, making Aunty flinch. "Look at this! How can you have denied me this all these years?"

Aunty turned away. "I was scared," she said softly. "I was scared that if I encouraged it, your mother would come for you. You don't want to be part of the world she's built over here, Stella."

Mam dropped her hand. "She can't be that bad . . . can she?"

"She is. Stella, she really is. You've no idea. You'd have had no chance with her . . . none. She'd . . . she'd have broken everything good about you."

"And now she has my dad," said Mup.

Aunty met her eyes and looked away again. "We don't know who has your dad," she said.

Tipper came racing into the clearing, Badger by his side.

"Mam! Mam!" barked Tipper. "We runned very fast and then we found you!" He skidded to a halt at the sight of the raven. "Oh," he said. "Bird."

Badger growled, and Tipper circled back to his side. "There's a tangledy bird," he said.

At the sight of the dogs, the raven had stopped fluttering, and he cowered wide-eyed in the leaves.

Mup touched his trembling back. "It's OK, Crow," she said. "This is just my family. My mam and aunty, my brother and my dog. They won't hurt you." The raven's feathers were stiff and glossy beneath her fingers. She could feel his heart hammering. He shot a bright, terrified glance her way. "I promise," she said. "No one here will hurt you."

"We need to leave, Stella," said Aunty. "That raven is very young. He's hardly likely to be out on his own. We can't risk his people finding us without knowing what to expect from them."

The raven moaned as Mam turned to look his way.

"It's OK," whispered Mup. "It's OK." But even she was frightened by the expression on her mother's face. When Mam came and snatched Crow—stone and all—from his huddle on the ground, the poor bird had barely time to squawk before he was shoved out of sight into the baby bag and slung onto Mam's back.

Mup watched, frozen for a moment, as Mam strode into the trees.

Aunty bobbed in her wake. "What exactly is your plan, Stella?"

"Well, until you offer me some information or useful advice, I'll just have to continue making things up as I go along."

"You're going to walk until you get to your mother's palace, is that it? Knock on the door? Demand she give your husband back?"

"If that's what it takes. Yes."

"Kidnapping ravens as you go?"

Mam huffed and marched on. Mup ran to catch up. Tipper bounced, yapping and eager, to her side. "Where's we going, Mup? Am we keeping the bird?"

"Just keep up, Tipper," said Mup, her attention fixed on the baby bag, which swayed on her mother's back. She didn't like to think of Crow inside, all tangled together with the stone and the string. She jogged closer to Mam. "Crow?" she whispered. "Are you OK?"

There was a small sobbing noise from the bag, then nothing more.

Mup glanced up at Mam. Her brows were creased in a firm, dark way which said, *Don't talk to me.*

Mup grimaced.

They strode on in tense silence, and Tipper soon got bored. He ran ahead. Mup watched him weave to and fro, copying Badger as he hunted scent on the path. Aunty was a fleeting shimmer, coming and going from sight as she drifted through patches of light and shade. Mam was cold and fierce and determined.

Is this really my family now? thought Mup. *That ghost, these dogs . . .* She glanced back up at her mam. *This witch?* She didn't even have to pinch herself to know the truth.

They walked all day, meeting no one and seeing nothing but trees. When the moon rose, full and knowing, into the network of branches above their heads, Mam called a halt. She and Mup gathered sticks and dry grass, like when they were camping, and built a tiny fire. Tipper flopped down into the leaves, panting, and Mup sat across the fire from him while Badger did a snuffling patrol of their surroundings. Aunty, nothing now but a small ball of light, glided up the nearest tree and roosted there like an owl.

Mam's eyes flashed to her as she struck a match to the tinder. "Are you all right up there, old lady?"

"I'm tired," whispered Aunty. "It's been a long day."

"I'm sorry we argued."

Aunty pulsed slightly: a kind of a weary shrug.

"Thank you for sticking around. I don't know what I'd have done without you when they came last night."

"Don't know what you'll do if they come again,

Stella. Don't fool yourself that you're strong enough to resist them." Mam tutted and snapped twigs into the fire, and Aunty sighed. "Don't know how much longer I can stay. Very tired. Feeling a little thin."

"Get some sleep," Mam said. She huddled into her jacket, frowning into the flames as they took hold of the wood. At her feet, Tipper snored, lax and golden and happy. Badger came and watched the fire awhile, his chin on his paws, then closed his eyes.

"Go asleep, Mup," said Mam.

Mup startled, surprised that Mam had known she was still awake. Had Mam known Mup was watching her? Had she felt Mup examining the shadows and highlights of her smooth, pale face?

"Do you know how to find Dad?" Mup asked softly.

Mam's dark eyes flickered in the firelight. She seemed to consider something a moment — whether or not to tell the truth, maybe — then said, "No."

"Are we just going to keep walking forever?"

"Until we get to a town or a road or something and Aunty can get her bearings. Apparently things have changed a lot since we were last here."

"And then we rescue Dad?"

Mam nodded.

"And then we all go home?"

Mam frowned. She looked down into the fire again. Mup felt a little thrill of anger, thinking she wouldn't answer the question, but then Mam said, quietly, "Would you want to go home, Mup?"

The anger turned to fear. "Of course I want to go home."

"Really? Back to homework and grocery shopping and television?" Mam glanced at Aunty's small light. There were snores coming from it, faint but steady. Mam leaned forward as if not wanting to disturb Aunty. "You felt what it was like to climb that tree, Mup. You don't want to lose that feeling, do you?"

"Aunty says it's dangerous here."

Mam spread her hands and allowed lightning to crackle between her fingers again. "Maybe we're fit for it," she whispered.

"Tipper is a dog here, Mam."

"Tipper is a baby. Who knows what he might like to be when he grows up."

"A dog, though?"

Her mother shrugged as if to say, *It's up to Tipper*.

"What about Crow?" asked Mup.

"Who?"

"Crow, Mam. The raven."

Her mother sighed.

"You can't leave him in that bag all night."

"He's fine, Mup. He's probably fast asleep in there, dreaming of worms. I'll decide what to do with him in the morning."

"It's cruel."

"It's necessary."

Mup tightened her arms and her jaw.

Mam surprised her by smiling. "Go to sleep, Mup," she said gently. And as if to set a good example, Mam lay down in the leaves next to the dogs, cushioned her head in her arms, and closed her eyes.

"Crow?"

"Leave me alone."

Mup glanced back at the flickering fire. Mam and Tipper and Badger were sleeping. Aunty snored in her tree. Quietly, Mup knelt by the bag, which still hung from the branch where Mam had left it.

"I just want to make sure you're OK in there. I . . . I thought I heard you crying."

"You thought wrong!" exclaimed the raven. "I never cry."

Mup smiled. "You're forgetting to rhyme," she whispered. "Aren't you meant to? Every time?"

"No need for poems now I've been arrested," he muttered. "One good thing about being a jail-bird: I won't have to bother hunting out no more bloody rhymes."

"You're not arrested, Crow."

"I'm not?"

"No. My mam's just worried you'll tell people where we are. She's only trying to keep me and Tipper safe."

There was a moment of silence from the bag. Then a round, bright eye appeared at the flap. Crow regarded her curiously. "What's that like, then?" he said at last.

"Pardon?"

"To have someone who cares if you're safe?"

He didn't sound so gruff now. He just sounded young and interested, and a little lonely.

"Don't you have a mam and dad, Crow?"

"I . . . I have a dad. He's gone, though. I miss him."

Mup leaned closer. "Oh, Crow. I'm sorry."

The round, bright eye blinked at her, then Crow pushed his head closer to the gap. "Mup . . . ?" he whispered. "Let me out."

Rebels, Ravens, and Cats

"I can't believe it," growled Mam, crunching her way through the leaves ahead. "I cannot believe she did that."

"She's just a child."

"After I told her. After I warned her."

Aunty sighed her transparent sigh and drifted luminously along behind.

"When I catch that raven," said Mam, "oh, the things I'll do to it."

Mup trudged miserably in their wake. When she had released Crow from the bag, she had been filled with sympathy and with certainty that it was the right thing to do. She'd had no clear idea of what might happen next, but there had been vague and cosy notions of whispered chats by the fire,

Mup magnanimously sharing the crust from her sandwiches, Crow's gratitude.

When Crow had stuck out his leg in wordless command that she untie him, she'd felt the smallest twinge of doubt. But she'd bent to the task, because who would want to be tied to a rock? The wool had recognized her touch and slithered away from the stone like water dribbling from a tap—all the beautiful crochet netting undoing itself in one easy release until it was just a length of scarlet tied to the bird's ankle.

Crow had leapt from her with a flurry of dark wings. Mup had shrunk back, and when she'd looked up he was gone. For a long time after, she'd searched the firelit branches for the glimmer of his eye, but she knew he'd fled.

Mup hugged herself in unhappiness, betrayed that he'd left without so much as a goodbye or a thank you. *But who could blame him?* she thought, glancing up at her furious mother striding through the morning sunshine. *In his shoes, I would have done the same thing.*

"You made Mammy scary," whispered Tipper accusingly. "Why am you so naughty?"

Mup felt very angry suddenly at just how unfair everyone was being. "It was mean!" she cried.

"Putting Crow in a bag like that. Tying him to a stone. It was cruel!"

"Cruel?" cried her mother, swinging around to face her. "He's a spy!"

"He's not a spy! He's just a . . ." For some reason Mup wanted to say "boy," but that wasn't right. "He's only young," she said. "And you put him in a bag!"

Her mother faltered, seemingly uncertain.

Aunty drifted impatiently in the background, scanning the trees. "We have to be careful here, Pearl," she said. "We have to keep ourselves safe."

"By tying up helpless birds and shoving them in bags?"

Aunty huffed. "It's not so easy to know what's helpless here and what is not."

But Mam was frowning thoughtfully at Mup.

"It wasn't right, Mam," said Mup softly.

Mam bent down so they were face to face. When had her skin become so smooth and pale? Had her eyes always been so dark? *Always*, thought Mup, with a start. *Mam has always looked like this*. It was as though Mam had spent her whole life out of focus, like a blurry photograph, and now—on this side of the border—Mup was seeing her clearly for the very first time.

Do I look different too? she thought.

Mam stared deep into Mup's eyes. She seemed to be searching for something there. For one moment Mup was terrified that her mam was going to ask, "Who *are* you?" But a fierce commotion broke out in the trees ahead, and Mam swung around, flinging her arm up to keep Mup behind her, and Mup felt loved by her again, and protected.

Aunty drifted back to them. Badger stepped in front of Tipper, and everyone listened. Something huge was smashing and crashing through the bushes out there. Someone was fighting in the undergrowth.

Silence fell. Then somewhere out of sight ahead, someone laughed.

Oh, what a terrible sound! It wasn't like a laugh at all, more the tinkling of some cruel bell in a frozen wilderness of ice. It made Mup want to crawl into her mother's pocket.

"We need to leave," whispered Aunty.

There was more crashing, that crystalline laugh again, and then somewhere out there in the trees Crow cawed, angry and defiant and obviously very afraid. Horrified, Mup took a step towards his voice. Her mother grabbed her arm, stopping her. Crow called again, desperate and helpless, and that laugh —

that terrible laugh — was all that answered him.

Mup met her mother's eyes. *We can't leave him.*

The next Mup knew they were stalking towards the noise together; she and her mam slipping smoothly through the bushes with the dogs at their heels and Aunty, a fierce ball of light, at their backs.

"Raggedy witches," warned Mup. She signalled the dogs to stay back, and she and Mam crouched low, peering through brightly coloured leaves at the four men and women who stood at the centre of the wood.

One of the man witches had his arm raised high over his head. He was holding the length of scarlet wool that trailed from Crow's ankle, and at the end of it Crow fluttered like a frenzied kite while the witches gazed up at him.

"My mother will kill you!" cawed Crow.

The witches laughed in detached amusement.

The one holding the string smiled as Crow desperately tried to fly away.

"My father will turn you into frogs!" he cawed.

With just a flicker of anger the witch yanked Crow from the air and dashed him to the ground. Leaves and feathers flew up at the impact, and the witches stepped back as a boy — no older than Mup — was revealed in the place where the raven should have been. Mup stared. Was that Crow? Gasping, the boy rolled onto his hands and knees, and Mup realized that, yes, it was most certainly Crow—there could be no doubting those large black eyes.

Crow's a boy, she thought—and somehow that didn't feel at all surprising.

"Well, well," said a witch. "It's the brat."

Crow, still dazed, tried to crawl away. Mup was shocked at how skinny he was, and how very scruffy when compared to his sleek raven form. His black hair stuck up in unkempt snarls, his old-fashioned frock coat and breeches and fancy shirt were all frayed and grubby. The witches followed as he scrabbled through the leaves, and Mup was overcome with sympathy again, and anger that anyone would treat him so badly.

"We should arrest you for unlawful speech," said one of the witches. "But tell us where your people are, and we will let you go free."

"Go suck a newt," gasped Crow, still crawling.

"Unlawful!" cried another witch. "Where are your rhymes?" She stamped onto the scarlet wool that trailed from Crow's ankle, and he jerked to a halt, sprawling face first into the leaves.

Crow let out a sob—just a tiny one—before

snarling and struggling to his knees. That was enough for Mup, and before her mother could stop her, before she'd even really thought about it, she had leapt to her feet and was dashing out into the clearing, yelling, *"You get away from my friend, you hear me? You leave my friend alone!"*

The witches lifted their terrible faces, and Mup slid to a crouching halt at their feet, spreading an arm across Crow's back and staring up into their horrible, dark, bottomless eyes.

"What a quaint and colourful little madam," murmured one of them. "What a glittering, tinselly, silly little scrap." The witch reached a pale hand — apparently fascinated by Mup's sparkly dress — and Mam yelled, "Get away from my daughter!"

The witches swung to see the new threat.

Mup bent over Crow's ankle, horrified at how the wool was biting into his scrawny flesh. It was barely visible, so deeply had it sunk — she hated to think how much it must be hurting him.

"Let me go!" snarled Crow, tugging free of her grip.

"Stop that, Crow!" Mup laid her hand on the wool. *Undo*, she urged.

The wool shivered, as if longing to obey, but uncertain that it should.

Behind her, Mam said, "I mean it. Come away from my daughter."

One of the witches said, "Who are you, to command officers of the queen?"

Magic crackled in the air. Leaves began to swirl up from the ground. Someone — not Mam — gasped in surprise and fear.

Crow clutched Mup's arm. "What is your mother doing?" he said. "She's standing *against* them. She's using *magic*! Is she mad?"

Abruptly, he turned his face to the treetops and cawed. It was a startling sound coming from a boy, but Mup forced herself to ignore it and whatever Mam was up to. She concentrated instead on the wool cutting cruelly into Crow's leg. *Undo!* she commanded again. *I don't care what Aunty wants, I won't have part of my favourite dress biting someone's foot off!* The wool relaxed beneath her hand and with an apologetic sigh coiled in scarlet loops on the ground.

Mup spun at last to face the witches. Leaves were whipping about her like a golden cyclone. Mup swatted them from her face, trying to see.

Crow, still cawing at the sky, lurched to his knees. As if in response to his desperate calling, a black shape shot from the trees above. It was a raven. Huge and strong, it knocked Mup aside as it swooped past. Just before the raven hit the ground it shook off its bird-shape and became a man. Tall and running, his long grey hair flying out behind him, the man stooped to snatch Crow into his arms. Without pause, he dashed away with him into the storm of leaves.

Across the fleeing man's shoulder, Crow kept cawing and cawing.

Harsh voices answered from the treetops, and the air darkened as more ravens swooped down. One of the raggedy witches turned from Mam and with a loathsome shudder became a cat. Teeth bared, she leapt at one of the ravens and brought it to the ground in a rage of claws and feathers. Screaming, the raven barely managed to struggle free. With an agonized cry, it flapped for the treetops, drops of scarlet falling from its wounded side.

Mup briefly saw her mother, striding through the frantic whirl of leaves. Her hands were outstretched, lightning flashing as she blasted a witch from her path. "Run, Mup!" she yelled. "Follow your aunty! I'll try and hold these creatures back."

Aunty's light bobbed into sight through the swirl of leaves. "This way!"

Mup tried to run to her, but a raggedy witch

staggered into her. It was the man witch who had treated Crow so cruelly. A raven was pecking at his eyes. The raggedy witch flung up his arm. His dark cloak billowed, and suddenly he too was a raven. The two enormous birds fluttered right in front of Mup's face, cawing and scratching. Their sharp claws scored scarlet trenches into each other's feathers.

Mam shot lightning at them, blasting them away from her daughter. "RUN!" she commanded.

Mup did as she was told. Looking back, she saw the lightning-charred ravens tumble apart. One of them launched itself desperately for the treetops; the other rolled, gasping, onto his side, a raggedy witch once more. Smoke poured from his cloak and hair.

"Come on!" cried Aunty from somewhere ahead in the maelstrom. "This way!"

"Where's Tipper?" cried Mup.

Tipper had rushed into the fray. Now he rolled into view, snapping in wild-eyed frenzy, thin lines of blood streaked across his muzzle. Mup grabbed the scruff of his neck. "This way, Tipper! This way! Follow Aunty!" She had to drag him for a moment before he realized who she was, then he followed of his own accord.

Aunty led them in the direction the man had

carried Crow. Mup thought she could still hear Crow faintly calling, but it was hard to know for sure over the sound of the cats howling and ravens cawing behind her.

"What about Mam?" she cried. She couldn't see her mother at all through the storm of leaves. When Mup tried to turn back for her, Aunty zapped her sharply with lightning. "Ow!" cried Mup. "Ow! OK! I'm moving."

Still herding Mup and Tipper forward, Aunty looked anxiously back. "Come on, Stella," she muttered. "Come on. Just run!"

They ran and ran, until Aunty suddenly stopped, and then they all stood, panting and listening. Mup went to ask about Mam again, but Aunty held up a transparent hand to shush her.

The forest was still, and breathlessly silent. The sound of fighting was gone. They were at the edge of a small, sunlit clearing. Just ahead of them, the grey-haired man had also come to a panting halt, Crow in his arms. The man was staring at Aunty in disbelief.

"Duchess?" he said.

Aunty squinted at the man's face as if unsure of who he was, then her expression opened in recognition. "Sealgaire," she whispered. "By grace. Is it really you?"

Before he could answer, there was a sound above them. Everyone flinched as dark shadows loomed overhead. The man snatched Crow to him, ready to run again. Mup grabbed Tipper.

"Is it witches?" Tipper barked. "Don't worry, Mup! I will bite them like I did the other witch. I will snap and crunch and . . ." He growled a fierce little puppy-growl.

Mup kept a hold of him, poised warily as huge ravens spiralled down from the sunlit treetops. Across the clearing, the man called Sealgaire relaxed, and Mup saw that these ravens were his friends. "It's OK, Tipper," she said as Sealgaire lowered Crow to the ground. "See? Crow isn't afraid of these people."

Indeed, Crow was staring up at the new arrivals with a kind of awe. They landed at Sealgaire's side, then rose to their feet as men.

"You came for me," Crow said in obvious disbelief. "You came to save me."

Sealgaire hushed him gently, his eyes once again fixed on Aunty. He seemed about to speak when his attention switched to the trees behind Mup.

He shrank back, and Mup spun to see what it was that had frightened him. It was only Mam, striding, frowning, through the trees, Badger at her heels. She came stalking past Mup and Tipper and Aunty and put herself between her children and the strangers.

"Mammy!" barked Tipper. "A bad cat scratched me, but I bited it! Then I ranned with Aunty and Mup to here!"

"Good boy," muttered Mam. "Mind the children, Badger," she said, and Badger — all hackles and teeth — took up guard at Mup and Tipper's side.

Mam's attention was focused on the men. There were five of them, not counting Sealgaire. All were dressed in the same old-fashioned manner as Crow, equally threadbare and faded, all with the same dark hair and large, dark, wary eyes. Some of them were very badly wounded indeed, and blood ran in shocking quantities from gashes and cuts. One man's eye was swollen completely shut. Another man leaned on a tree as if unable to put weight on his leg.

Mam, apparently surprised at their condition, straightened from her defensive crouch. She lowered her sparking hands. "Oh," she said. "I was angry that you didn't stay and help me protect my children . . . but I now see you did your best."

The men exchanged glances. One of them gestured for Sealgaire to speak.

Sealgaire bowed, seemed to think a moment, then carefully rhymed:

> "Madam, you were brave and good,
>
> To aid our boy-child in this wood."

Crow, suddenly furious, exclaimed, "Aid me? Sealgaire, she put me in a bag!"

As one, the men glared at him, and Crow flushed. His face screwed up in concentration. Speaking slowly, and with much thought between words, he managed:

> "She . . . she went and put me in a bag,
>
> She's a rotten, nasty hag!"

Sealgaire tutted:

> "Try and have some manners, Crow,
>
> You've caused more trouble than you know."

"Who are you?" Mam asked him.

Sealgaire regarded her with a strange mixture of fear and bright-eyed hope.

> "Madam, if I may be so bold to ask,
>
> Are you the heir returned at last?"

One of the other men hissed and gripped Sealgaire's arm to silence him. But Sealgaire continued to address Mam in growing excitement.

"Has the duchess brought you home,

To take your place upon the throne?"

He seemed about to go on, but a trio of cats ran from the trees and he turned to them instead, delighted and relieved at their arrival.

One of the cats, sleek and noble with pale-grey fur, furiously outran the others in her hurry to cross the clearing. Aunty straightened at the sight of her. "Fírinne!" she whispered.

"Do you know that cat, Aunty?" asked Mup, but Aunty didn't reply. She just continued regarding the angry feline with what Mup could only interpret as longing and sorrow.

The grey cat yowled as she and her companions reached the men. "Look at you! You're bleeding! You're hurt! Oh, I'm sorry it took so long to get to you. I can't believe you went after him! Oh, that boy!" She prowled around Sealgaire to get to Crow, who drew back, scowling. "What is wrong with you?" hissed the cat. "Will you never learn?"

"Fírinne." Sealgaire smiled. Holding out a placating hand, he said:

"We snatched the boy and quickly fled,

The enforcers shan't find where we've hid.

More than that, Oh, so much more,

Look who has walked back through our door."

He gestured to Aunty.

The cat's eyes widened in momentary shock. "Duchess," she said. "You have returned."

"Fírinne," said Aunty. "Oh, my friend. It is so good to see you."

The cat did not seem to agree. "Returned but in a very reduced state, I see. I had not thought you would be one of those who refuse to cross the fragile veil. Troubled by an uneasy conscience?" The cat smiled, but there was no warmth to it.

Aunty flushed slightly and looked down at her transparent body.

To Mup, it seemed that Aunty's discomfort pleased the cat. She arched and rose and, in one sinuous movement, transformed into a graceful woman of sixty or so, with long silver hair and beautiful, though faded, clothes. The rest of the cats also transformed into women. They went to support the wounded men. All of them gathered in a watchful group at the silver-haired woman's back, and Mup guessed that she was their leader.

"We need to run, Fírinne," said one of the

91

women. "It's not possible they could have evaded the queen's enforcers this easily."

"Mam hid us," said Mup. She paused as over half a dozen strangers switched their gaze to her. "She . . . she stormed up all the leaves and confused the raggedy witches."

"Raggedy witches?" said Fírinne.

"It's what she calls my sister's creatures," said Aunty.

"They can't follow us because Mam hid us as we ran," explained Mup. "Isn't that right, Mam?"

Mam nodded. She and Fírinne regarded each other with suspicious curiosity.

"We're safe," said Mup. "Aren't we, Mam?"

"I don't know," said Mam. "I don't know how things work here. No one ever explained any of this to me—except to say I need to be quiet and do as I'm told."

"We are not safe," said Fírinne. "Whomever the queen wants, her enforcers find. It only takes one unlawful word or deed for them to sniff you out."

Mup stepped closer, entranced by Fírinne's fierce expression. Her eyes were just as piercing as a raggedy witch's, just as unsettling, though sparking and vibrant—not crushing and cold as theirs had been.

Fírinne dragged her attention from Mam and

looked down at Mup. Something about her seemed to startle Fírinne—as though she were seeing Mup properly for the first time. Gently, she touched Mup's red coat and sparkly dress. "Oh, child," she whispered. "Aren't you brave to shine so bright in this disapproving world?"

"Are you and your friends witches?" asked Mup.

Fírinne's eyebrow quirked, as if Mup had just asked the most amusing question. "Of course we are," she said. "Aren't you?"

Witches! thought Mup in astonishment. "But . . . you're not like those others."

This hardened the woman's face a little. "I should hope not," she said.

"Fírinne is an old friend of mine," Aunty told Mup. "These are her tribe, Clann'n Cheoil—the music people."

"What's left of Clann'n Cheoil. After your sister's doings."

Again, Aunty looked uncomfortable. "My sister's doings were never any of my business, Fírinne. And even if they were"—she gestured to her body—"you can see I'm little more than a memory now."

The woman huffed. "You've been nothing but a memory for decades."

Sealgaire came to Fírinne's elbow and murmured:

"The duchess has returned the heir,
The queen will soon find out she's here.
If we don't wish to end in jail,
We should consider setting sail."

Fírinne eyed Mam again. "Are you here to start a war? It's what your mother always feared—that you'd be back after years of preparation to wrest her from the throne."

Mam chuckled bitterly. "Preparation," she huffed. "The only thing I've been preparing all this time are dinners and bottles and beds."

Fírinne frowned in confusion. "Well, whatever your purpose, I don't want you dragging my people into it. They've suffered enough." She glanced at Crow. "As for you, child, you're getting to be more trouble than you're worth. Next time we should just leave you to the mercy of the queen's creatures . . . regardless of what Sealgaire has to say."

Crow went to retort and the woman flung up her hand. "Stop! No one has any patience for finishing your rhymes today, and we can all do without your unlawful speech drawing more of the queen's enforcers down on us."

Crow jutted his chin in defiance.

"Look at him!" cried one of the clann. "He's not

even sorry!" She rounded on Crow. "You're the reason these men are injured. Thanks to you we'll probably have to move on *again*. Why can't you stay where we put you instead of wandering off all the time?"

Crow began to shake, his fists and face screwed up in rage.

Sealgaire stepped between him and the others.

"*Crow,*" he said gently.

"*Best hold your tongue.*

There'll be time to talk when day is done."

Fírinne made a noise of disgust. "Enough of this. We must flee." She stalked away into the trees, and her people followed her.

After a moment's hesitation, Mam strode after them. Tipper and Badger ran to her heels, and with a sigh, Aunty followed.

"Aren't you coming, Crow?" asked Mup.

He regarded her from the centre of the clearing, his skinny chest rising and falling with unspoken anger. She waited as the others got further and further away.

Eventually, she said, "Please don't stay here on your own, Crow. Please come with us."

And finally, as if losing a great battle with himself, Crow joined her, and they followed the adults through the woods.

Clann'n Cheoil

Mup and Crow ran to catch up.

The music people kept their human forms as they marched through the woods. They did nothing to deter Mup's family from following them. Mam and Aunty held a muttered conversation as they stalked on their tail.

"Clann'n Cheoil are good people," said Aunty, as if to reassure herself. "At least, they used to be good people."

"Don't care who they are," said Mam. "As long as I get the information I need to rescue Daniel."

"I'm sure they'll help all they can, seeing how we saved their boy."

Mam grimaced. "I'm not sure they're all that happy to have him back."

Mup glanced at Crow. He was limping badly and there was blood on his stocking where the wool had cut his flesh. She thought it was odd that no one—not even her mother—had thought to check his leg or ask if he was all right. Admittedly, he was scowling in that off-putting manner and his hands were clenched up into fists, but Mup had never known an adult to let something like that stop them from fussing—especially not if a kid had blood on them.

"Are *Clann'n Cheoil* your family, Crow?" she asked.

Crow's mouth squirmed about, his brow creasing as he searched for words. He must not have managed to find any because he just shook his head.

Mup thought a while. Then she said, "If you're having a hard time, I could help you with the rhyme."

Crow slammed to a halt, his whole body suffused with mortified rage.

"*I'll find my own words!*" he cried.

"*I don't need you to . . . I don't need anyone to . . .*"

He made a frustrated sound again, his face growing red as he searched for a rhyme to end his sentence with. Mup said nothing, and Crow spun abruptly away from her. He went back to limping through the leaves. Mup walked with him.

"I'm sorry," she murmured. And she was too.

Not because she had tried to help—why should she be sorry for that?—but because of all the words she could see bottled up inside him with no way of getting out, and because of how upset that seemed to make him. Tentatively, she asked, "Will . . . will the raggedy witches come back now? Because you didn't rhyme?"

Crow clumped on, and Mup thought he maybe wouldn't answer her, but after a while he said, "If my . . . if my meanings stay . . ." He grunted in frustration, and then thumped his chest as if to illustrate his point.

"Inside?" asked Mup.

He nodded.

"*If my meanings stay*"—he thumped his chest—
"*Her people keep away.*"

Mup stopped walking. "Crow, are you saying that if people can't understand you properly, the witches will leave you alone? Is that what the rule is for? To stop people understanding each other? To make it harder for people to talk?"

Crow huffed. "Some people. Rebel people."

"That's terrible, Crow. That's a terrible thing to do to anyone."

Crow's expression softened as if in surprise at Mup's attitude. He nodded.

Up ahead, Tipper snuffled the trail, copying Badger with babyish self-importance. Mup considered him a moment, then said quietly, "I think my brother bit a raggedy witch."

Crow stared at her in horror.

"He has scratches on his nose," said Mup. "And I can't be sure, but I think he said he bit a cat. Tipper's just a baby, Crow. I don't think he even understands what he did. But he's a big strong dog here. He's not used to being a dog. And . . . and you've seen how sharp his teeth are."

They stood watching as the adults strode further and further away, Tipper happily trotting with them, his golden tail a banner, waving his happiness. What would happen to him if people knew? If you got thrown in jail just for using the wrong words, what would the punishment be for biting one of the queen's witches?

Crow whispered, "Are you sure?"

Mup shook her head. How could she be?

"If I had the teeth, I'd do the same," admitted Crow.
"I'd bite them all. I'd chew and maim."

You had no trouble rhyming that, thought Mup.

"I don't think it would be a good idea if folk knew Tipper did this, Crow."

Crow nodded in fierce agreement. He grabbed and earnestly shook Mup's hand. It was as if he were trying to put all his unspoken words into that gesture, and Mup understood it was his way of telling her he'd keep Tipper's secret. She squeezed his fingers, suddenly very glad that she'd shared her fears with him and that she'd released him from the bag and gone to rescue him from the witches.

After a while, they came to a wide space in the woods where the leaf-littered ground sloped down to a river and sunlight. There were small wooden caravans and little tents dotted about. All were painted in what had once been beautiful colours but—like the clothes of the people themselves—they were faded to the faintest memory of their previous glory. Campfires hazed the air and fragrant steam drifted from round-bellied pots, reminding Mup how hungry she was. The place looked deserted, but as Fírinne led her people into camp, the men threw back their heads and cawed. Within moments cats were slinking from the bushes and ravens were wheeling down from the sky. Soon men and women filled the camp.

"Are there no other children here?" asked Mup.

Crow shrugged, limping onwards.

"Once there were children, long ago,
No children now, that's all I know.
Too risky for a rebel's band,
To keep their children . . ."

He thought hard.

"To keep their children . . ."

"Close at hand?"

"I would have got that!"

Mup sighed. "Sorry, Crow."

He thumped his chest again.

"To safer place I will not go.
Though Sealgaire tries to make me so.
I stay to fight,
And find my dad.
I'd rather that than . . . than . . ."

His pride deflated in the fruitless search for rhyme. Angrily, he kicked a stone.

Mup grimaced in silent sympathy.

Anxious glances were thrown at the newcomers as the music people gathered together at the heart of the camp. Shocked exclamations greeted news of the altercation with the raggedy witches. *You fought officers of the queen? What if they recognized you? There'll be a bounty on us all!*

Mup noticed the men did little of the talking. Most simply listened as the women vented everyone's distress.

"Is it only your men that must speak rhyme, Crow?"

> "*Queen's rules change from clann to clann.*
>
> *For us, she ties the tongue of man.*
>
> *Hard to find true harmony,*
>
> *When half our voices are not free.*"

In the crowd, a woman asked anxiously of Fírinne's crew, "Is it possible you were not recognized? If you stayed in animal form—"

"We were rescuing the brat! Of course we were recognized!"

Crow became the focus of many a furious glare.

"This is all your fault, Sealgaire," cried one of the women. "It's you keeps risking all for a child who is no longer one of our own. His father is *gone*. His mother has *severed from him*. He's no longer *wanted!*"

Sealgaire spread his hands in an angry gesture that clearly meant, *Do not talk that way.*

But another woman said, "His parents were

nothing but trouble, and he's been nothing but trouble since you took him in. Why must we keep chasing after him? Stop asking us to risk our lives every time he runs off."

Sealgaire turned in appeal to Fírinne, and she shrugged unhappily as if she thought the others might be right.

Once again, Mup was struck with just how unfair it was that no one seemed to care about Crow. "Well, that's just wrong," she said, causing all the adults to pause and look at her. "Poor Crow. Why would you be so mean?"

"She's right," said Aunty. "What kind of people are you, to leave a child to the mercy of those . . . creatures?"

Fírinne huffed. "You left us at their mercy," she said.

"I had a child to protect."

"And the rest of us didn't, I suppose? Did you pay a moment's thought to the young you left behind? You've no idea the kind of life they've had to live under your sister's reign. They've had to grow up hard—and they will grow harder still if things do not change. You cannot judge us for what we've had to become in your absence."

"There are other boroughs in the Glittering Land," said Aunty. "Why not leave if things were so bad?"

"Why *should* we leave? Witches Borough is our home!"

"*Besides,*" added Sealgaire quietly,

"*if everyone sings a leaving song,*

Who will right your sister's wrongs?"

Aunty went very quiet at that and seemed to grow even more transparent. She dropped her eyes and drifted slightly back from the conversation.

Mam's gaze had been hopping from Aunty to Fírinne as they argued. Now she spoke softly from the background. "This is not helping me find my husband. That's all I'm interested in here."

"*No point asking them to find him!*" shouted Crow.

"*They never mean a word they say,*

They promise help, then walk away!"

"Crow." Sealgaire sighed. "Enough." And he manhandled the angry boy across the clearing to the steps of a caravan, where he left him sitting and scowling at anyone who looked at him.

Mup thought he looked terribly lonely there.

Despite Aunty's obvious discomfort, Mam began a murmured conversation with Fírinne's people. Tipper snuffled around the tense knot of adults with merry enthusiasm, attempting to lick hands and sniff into pockets. The scratches on his muzzle were a vivid, bloody brand on his face, and Mup thought it was horribly obvious that they were cat scratches.

"Tipper," she called, patting her leg as though he really were a dog. "Tipper, come here and we'll go sit with Crow."

Tipper lolloped over in slobbering delight. "Mammy is asking the cat-ladies where Daddy is!" he barked.

All excitement, he went to run off again. Mup grabbed his scruff and drew him to Crow's lonely perch on the caravan steps.

"Would you like a sandwich, Tipper?" she asked. "Look . . . I have some here."

She rooted in her backpack for the sandwiches she'd made at home. They were very squashed and sad and ordinary-looking in their cling-film wrapper, but Tipper almost somersaulted at the sight of them.

"Cheese!" he barked. "Oh, cheese! Cheese! Cheese!"

"Shh," said Mup, unwrapping the misshapen bread. She held a sandwich up, just out of his reach. "Sit!" she said.

Tipper sat, his tail whisking, his tongue lolling, his eyes riveted on the food.

"You can only eat here, Tipper, OK? No going over to where Mammy is."

"She's making the angry people promise to find Daddy!" barked Tipper.

Crow sat straighter at that, his scowl gone.

Tipper barked "cheese" again as if Mup might have forgotten the sandwich drooping limply in her fingers. She began to feed it to him, just a little at a time to keep him in place. Crow was staring at her, his eyes wide and hopeful and brimming now with a raw desire to speak.

"Crow," she said. "We'll never be able to talk if you don't let me help you. Try and find the words, and let me help you if I can."

Crow thumped his chest. Huge tears in his eyes. "I want to find my dad too. To save him. Help him, just like you! No one here will help me. They used to be his friends!" Crow leapt to his feet, his rage not allowing him to sit still any longer. "Now they won't even say his name!"

At the sound of his voice, some of the clann looked over.

"Toraí!" Crow shouted at them. "Dad's name is *Toraí!*"

"Use your rhymes," they replied, "or you'll be sorry!"

Mup dragged him down to sit by her again.

"Why won't they help me?" he cried. "Why?"

Mup didn't know. She'd always had someone to help when she'd needed it—her aunty or her mam. She couldn't imagine calling out like that and no one caring. "But, Crow," she said, "you need to be careful to rhyme. Otherwise the witches will come."

His round eyes glittered at her, and Mup saw fear there, but also some kind of sly and frantic desperation.

"Would being arrested be so bad," he whispered,

"If the witches took me to my dad?"

"Oh, Crow. Do they have your dad too?"

"They came and took him in the night . . ."

He paused—obviously upset.

"That . . . that must have been an awful sight," said Mup.

It felt wrong making a rhyme of such a terrible memory—it felt like she were making a joke of it. Sure enough, Crow pulled free of her grip, and turned away. Mup thought again how cruel this law was; how much it robbed from someone, to make them bury their feelings in the hunt for the best or safest word. She put her hand on Crow's back.

"I want my dad," he whispered.

"Me too."

"Dad spoke against the law of rhyme.

He's been a prisoner since that time.

Tell me, what did your dad do

To get him thrown in prison too?"

Mup frowned. "I don't think he did anything. He's just a nice man who fixes oil rigs. But look, Crow, I'll help you find your dad."

He spun to stare at her.

"If the raggedy witches took both our dads, they might be in the same place," said Mup. "When we rescue my dad, Mam and I can help you rescue yours."

Crow pulled Mup closer.

"I don't trust your mam. But I trust you.

Let's work in secret, just us two."

"And me?" cried Tipper, looking up from the last of the sandwiches. "Me can help?"

Crow smiled, a completely foreign and charming expression on his storm cloud of a face.

"Yes, you too, little brother.

But no need to tell this to your mother."

Mup felt a twinge of unease. "Crow, Mam is OK. You'll see. Just give her a chance and—"

But Crow was pulling her to her feet and enthusiastically dragging her down the steps and around the side of the caravan, out of sight of the others.

"We'll make dance magic, me and you,

Like in old days, two by two!"

Mup jerked to a halt, unsure. She glanced back at the camp. Mam had her back to them, Badger sitting obediently at her feet. She was talking intently to the glowering clann, paying no heed to her children's antics.

"What is 'dance magic,' Crow?" Mup asked.

He retreated behind his scowl, as if he suspected Mup of looking for excuses to go back on her promises.

"It's what clann used to do to work together,

Cheek by cheek, fur by feather.

To seal a bond, it is a must,

It says, 'We're friends,'

It says, 'We trust.'"

"Oh! Like making a pact? Like in school, when we spit on our palm and shake hands and say, 'Deal'?"

Crow recoiled in disgust.

"Urgh!" he cried. *"Spit? By my tall hat,*

Dance magic's not at all like that!"

He was so delightfully revolted that Mup had to laugh. "OK, Crow," she said. "I won't make you spit. Let's dance!"

In the quiet spaces behind the camp, at the back of the caravans, Crow spun in the bright leaves, his arms above his head. He was transformed with happiness. Not just smiling now, but grinning, the wild nest of his hair a jolly exclamation point on top of his head.

"Do what I do only opposite!" he cried.

"Floposite, moposite, toposite, loposite!" barked Tipper, lolloping about him in a big circle.

"*Arms up!*" sang Crow to Mup.

"*I sway left and you sway right,*

Dancing, dancing with all our might."

He looked absolutely ridiculous, prancing about waving his arms. But as he swayed and spun and grinned up at the sky, Mup felt a small shiver growing in the air: a little tickle within her chest and within the leaves at her feet. As if the ground were trying to sing to her. As if she were a dance waiting to happen. As if the world were all ashimmer with secret colours ready to shine if only she'd lift her arms.

Crow caught her eye as he came around from one of his clumsy turns and he knew at once she could feel the magic. The smile he gave her was so delighted that Mup lifted her arms and started to dance.

Oh, the colours!

All the colours!

Is this what being a witch is like? thought Mup. If so, it was lovely. Like when she'd climbed the tree, it was perfect and natural and good.

The leaves were gold beneath her feet. The grass a searing green. The blue of the sky roared overhead. Tipper's face glowed. And Crow—his previously faded clothes a sunburst of yellow and red—danced and danced in the glorious evening light, laughing, free and happy, as Mup spun with him.

First this way, then that, she spun, casting spangles of light from her dress, her coat a scarlet blur. In step with Crow. In step with Tipper. Weaving the threads of this faded world tight, then tighter still to make a bond that said, *Together, friends, always.*

And then—secondary to all this joyful togetherness, as if the world were unfolding a present for Mup alone to see—all the paths of the world opened out like a flower blossoming at her feet: all destinations possible or probable spread before her like a glittering net thrown over the world. All Mup had to do was concentrate and she would know the way anywhere, she could find anything, she could—

"NO!"

A frantic cry, a panicked hand on Mup's shoulder, and the dance came crashing down. The colours receded as Crow was pulled one way and Mup the other. She felt the magic tear as surely as a sheet of paper, and with the same sharp ripping sound. They were surrounded by adults.

"What have you done?" someone shouted.

Mup was dragged, stumbling, back to the heart of the camp.

"They were making outlaw magic!" cried a woman. "The heir's child and the brat!"

Sealgaire's face dipped low before Mup, a portrait of concern and anxiety, before he straightened and became just one more jostling adult. Mam gripped Mup's shoulder and pulled her near as the clann panicked around them.

"What do we do?"

"Flee! Flee before her witches come!"

"Whistle up the horses! Quick!"

Someone cuffed Crow's ear and flung him up the steps of a small blue caravan. Mup went to run after him. Mam dragged her back, but a voice said, "She'd be safer inside the *cáirín*, madam," and Mam released her to run up the faded steps, Tipper at her heels.

Mup was astounded to find Crow grinning in triumph—even as he clutched his aching ear.

"They didn't like that, did they?" he said.

Outside, the terrified *clann* began frantically breaking camp. Fires were stamped down. Goods were flung into caravans. Washing was ripped from lines. There were no horses, but one of the *clann* whistled up a wind which at first circled and spun and then settled between the shafts of each caravan until every vehicle was harnessed to its own small tornado, shivering and ready to go.

Mam watched all this from the base of the caravan steps. She shook her head at the chaos. "What were you up to, Mup Taylor?"

Mup could still feel the dance magic tingling in her hands like pins and needles; could still feel it fizzing in her spine. She jutted her chin. "Crow and I were only making a promise to help find each other's dads. I don't see what's wrong with that. The queen must be a *horrible* person if she won't let people do a lovely bit of magic like that."

The corner of Mam's mouth twitched upwards. "You looked like you were having fun, anyway," she said. "I didn't know magic could be fun."

"It's no fun for Crow to get hit on the ear, Mam! Someone should tell these people they can't hit little kids. You should tell them."

Mam took a long, lingering look at the boy standing in the shadows, then back at her daughter. "I have things to discuss with Fírinne. I'll be travelling in her caravan. Your aunty wants you to come travel with us. She thinks you'd be safer that way."

Mup huffed. "I'll stay with Crow, thank you very much. In case anyone else feels like hitting him on the ear."

The twitch at the corner of Mam's mouth became a brief smile. "That's my girl," she said. "Keep yourself out of trouble, Mup. Take care of your little brother." With that, she clamped her coat tight against the swirling leaves and strode off to mount the steps of another caravan, where Fírinne waited at the door.

Sealgaire came to stand in Mam's place. He stared at Crow and Mup, as if there were a litany of things he'd like to say to them, if only he could. Mup thought he looked more sad than angry — heartsick almost.

"Such colours you danced," he said softly. "I'd forgotten . . ." He shook his head, words failing him, and gestured at the faded wooden steps. He said:

"Take in the stairs and shut the door.

We cannot stay here anymore."

Sealgaire remained silent as they lifted the steps into the tiny interior, then he shut the door. Mup and Crow and Tipper crowded together at the little stained-glass windows, watching as the others pulled away from camp. Sealgaire took his place on the driver's seat of their own caravan, and soon they were following the small train of faded wagons into the trees.

"Where are we going?" Mup asked Crow.

He scowled out through the blue and yellow glass.

"They have no plan, just 'up and go.'

To run and hide is all they know.

How can they hope to set things right,

If they never stand and fight?"

Mup pressed her face to the window, her eyes on the fleeing clann. She couldn't help but think how awful the raggedy witches must be if grown men and women would rather pick up their homes and run than stand and face them.

Outlaw Magic

The journey seemed to last forever, with nothing but trees and golden leaves to be seen from the little stained-glass windows of the caravan. Crow peered through the panes as one tree gave onto another and one leaf-muffled path wound onto the next. It was impossible to have a conversation with him, and Mup began to wish she'd gone with her mother, where—despite almost certainly being accused of eavesdropping—she might have learned something about the plan to rescue Dad.

Tipper soon fell asleep, and out of boredom, Mup set about examining the interior of what Crow called the *cáirín*. It was a beautifully designed little home with a place for everything, and everything neat and gleaming in its place. A kettle, a stove, a lantern, a cupboard, a little built-in bed with steps up to it. Mup felt she could have explored the tiny place for hours and still not have discovered a fraction of its delightful secrets.

"Is this Sealgaire's home, Crow?"

The boy huffed, his round black eyes still fixed on the road ahead.

"No. It is my mother's.

Sealgaire minds it. He's her brother."

"You have a mother?" At Crow's dark look, Mup blushed. "Sorry," she said. "Of course you do. It's just, the way you talk about her. I assumed she was dead."

"Dead?"

Crow thought about this a moment, then shrugged as if he didn't care.

"Maybe yes, maybe no.

I never see her as I . . ."

He made a movement with his hand, something small getting taller.

". . . never see her as I grow."

"Does she work away?" asked Mup sympathetically. "That's why I never see my dad much. He works away. On oil rigs. In other countries."

Crow turned to her for the first time since the journey began, interested. "What is 'other countries'?"

117

"You know. Somewhere far away." She made an aeroplane motion with her hand. "You need to fly there."

Puzzled, Crow looked from her soaring hand to Tipper, asleep on the floor at their feet.

"Your father flies?

He is like Crow?

Then how is little brother so?"

"How is Tipper . . . so?"

"So!" Crow gestured in frustration to the sleeping puppy. *"So!"*

"You mean . . . a dog?"

Crow nodded.

"How is father this, and small boy that?

There are no rules, like 'Man is Raven,' 'Woman is Cat'?"

"Rules . . . ?" Mup was stumped, but before she could ask what Crow meant, the caravan came to a sudden halt.

Crow turned from her again and pressed his nose to the glass.

"As I spy," he whispered,

"Men are coming from the sky."

Mup peered out in time to see Sealgaire leave the cáirín and cross to join the others, who had nervously descended from their vehicles. They were gathering around a trio of strange men who were just that moment transforming from ravens. Crow seemed startled by the newcomers' human form.

"Speirling, *as my name is Crow!*

Castle folk, bad *to know!"*

"They live in the castle with the queen?" said Mup. She pressed her own nose to the window. "They don't look like raggedy witches."

"*They live in a castle,*" muttered Crow, jostling her aside to get a better view.

"*Not the castle.*

How is your mother meant to rule,

When you ask such questions like a fool?"

"You can't learn if you don't ask questions, Crow," said Mup mildly, elbowing her way back in. "And Mam's just Mam. She's not interested in ruling anything."

Mam stepped down from Fírinne's caravan, Aunty's ghost a blue light at her shoulder. Mup watched in fascination as the newcomers—sharp-featured, haughty men—knelt before her mother as if she were a queen.

"*Great and gracious Majesty,*" they said,

"*We, the Speirling, bow to thee.*"

Crow's mouth dropped open in shock.

"By my tall hat!

Since when must Speirling speak like that?"

"Do *Speirling* not normally need to rhyme?" asked Mup.

Crow shook his head.

"Only rebels need to rhyme.

And they must do it all the time."

Mup shrugged. "These must be rebels then."

Outside, Fírinne laughed in bitter amusement at the kneeling men. "Oh, the *Speirling*," she said. "Never happy without some haughty royal to bow to."

The sharp-faced men snapped her an angry look.

"Better to bow than live like ye,

In coarse and tumbling chaos.

At least royal law brings dignity,

And order to the masses."

"Royal law dictates how we should walk and talk and sing and dress!" cried Fírinne. "How does any of that give us dignity? How does any of it make our lives better? It's all just the queen's way of making people afraid! Of making us ashamed of what we once were, so she can continue denying us the magic we are all born with!"

"Shh, Fírinne," said Aunty, as if the trees, or

the stones, or the air around them might carry her friend's angry words to ungentle ears.

"Oh, you hush," snapped Fírinne. "All these years, these people stood aside as your sister squashed others down. As long as their kind were safe, everyone else could rot as far as the *Speirling* were concerned."

She turned again to the kneeling men. "But you finally fell from the queen's good graces, huh? What did you do? Sing the wrong song? Like the wrong poem? Use a bit of outlaw magic? And now you want someone new in her place. Now, after she's spent years hurling your fellow citizens into the dark. Well, damn you for that! Damn you! Do you think the *clann* will follow anyone you choose to give a crown to? You'd only saddle us with a new tyrant!"

The tall woman spat contemptuously and stalked away. Mup pressed her face to the window glass, trying to keep her in sight. As Fírinne passed Aunty's ghost, she hissed, "How good it must feel, Duchess, to have yet another queen in the family for people to bow and scrape to."

"I am not a queen," said Mam. But Mup thought she looked very regal when she said it, and the kneeling *Speirling* only bowed their heads lower. One of them held up a scroll of paper. None of the clann seemed inclined to take it, so Mam plucked it from his hand. Her face grew paler and sterner as she read.

Finally Fírinne could stand it no longer. "Oh, put us out of our misery, for grace. Tell us what it says!"

Mam lowered the paper. "You're right," she said to Fírinne. "They want me to fight my mother and take her place on the throne. They—"

"This is not your fight!" cried Aunty's ghost, snatching Mam's sleeve. "I kept you away from all that!"

The kneeling men rose urgently to their feet.

"*Majesty!*" they pleaded.

"*Restore your monarchy.*

Do not abandon us to tyranny!"

They gestured at Aunty.

"*Would you leave us,*

As she has done,

To the mercy of the other one?"

Mup turned to Crow in confusion. "What are they talking about? What about my dad?"

"*Talk, talk, talk,*" he said.

"*They're all the same.*

They'll talk and argue and squawk and shout,

Till your poor dad's forgot about."

"Never!" cried Mup, and she burst from the cáirín,

shouting, "Hey! *Hey!* We're here to rescue my dad!" She ran to her mother's side. "Mam! You don't care about being some queen, right? You just want Dad, right? You want to rescue Dad and come home!"

There were mutterings of consternation: men clucked and women hissed. In the midst of it all Mam looked down at Mup from what seemed a very great height. She lightly touched her daughter's cheek. Her fingers were cold and they buzzed, not unpleasantly, against Mup's skin. Mam's eyes swam with depths Mup had never before witnessed or suspected.

"Are those my only choices, little person?" Mam asked. "Queen or home? Two singular things, fractured and separate from each other?"

"What? Mam, what do you mean?"

But Mam's fingers had tightened on Mup's shoulder, and she turned to face the *Speirling.*

"Where is my husband?" she asked, her voice cold and somehow eternal, coming from above Mup's head. "Obviously it's you and not my mother who took him. Hoping to lure me here. Hoping — like everyone else — to control me."

The haughty men shifted uncomfortably.

"M-majesty, *without our women, our tongues are dull.*
We have not the words to explain in full . . ."

"It takes no skill to rhyme with 'yes' or 'no,'" snapped Mam. "Have you my husband or not?"

"We . . ." they said. *"That is . . ."*

They looked again at one another, and then said:

"Certain factions of the Speirling Clann
May have waylaid Your Highness's man.
But, Majesty, it was not us.
In this fact we pray you'll trust.
We —"

Mam silenced them with a raised hand. "Bring Daniel here," she ordered. "Now."

"Majesty, that is not a simple task.
Where your man is, we did not ask.
We are but messengers, we three.
To find your man we'd have to —"

"Oh good grace!" cried Mam, turning to Fírinne. "What are they trying to tell me?'

"That they don't personally have your husband, nor do they know where he is. Typical *Speirling*. They're always plotting, yet they always manage to stay just on the right side of the queen — mostly because they'd sell each other out in a heartbeat. The right hand never knows what the left is doing with them, so that if the queen tortures one of them they won't have too much information to give away.

Aren't I right, gentlemen? *Speirling* never trust each other not to *tattle*."

The *Speirling* gave her the hardest of looks.

> *"Only those who have not suffered at the hands of the queen,*
> *Would jest at the prospect of being made to scream."*

To Mup's surprise, Fírinne looked ashamed.

A sly look replaced the coldness on the *Speirling's* faces. One of them stepped forward and, as if offering the *clann* a poisoned apple, held out his hand.

> *"To find the heir's husband we might put out a call,*
> *Though it would mean raising our voices, one and all."*

Clann'n Cheoil drew back as if the *Speirling* had threatened to bite them.

"Choral magic," whispered someone. Mup could not figure out if they had spoken in fear or in longing — the expression on their faces was so complicated.

"Choral magic is unlawful," whispered another, with the same reluctant yearning.

"It . . . it would draw her witches down on us for sure," said another.

"It's been years since I've done choral magic," said another.

"Do you remember . . . ?"

"I remember."

People began murmuring all at once. Sealgaire and Fírinne locked eyes across the shifting, restless crowd. Mup felt that they were having a conversation without words: the two of them trying to come to some momentous decision.

Crow was scowling from face to conflicted face, his expression a bitter little twist of scorn. Mup pushed between the adults to get to him. "What are they talking about, Crow? Are they going to help find my dad?"

He shook his head and patted her arm in sympathy.

"Sadly, girl who is my friend,

You must allow all hope to end.

These folk would never risk themselves

To save your dad who is not—"

"We will do it," said Fírinne.

Crow gaped up at her, his skinny body lax with shock.

"They'll do it! They'll do it!" yelled Mup, so happy that she capered about a bit before remembering to ask, "Do what, though? Crow, what will they do? How will it save Dad?"

"No!" hissed one of the clann, yanking Crow away from her. "We're still fleeing this brat's last act

126

of outlaw magic. You've no idea the danger we'd be putting ourselves in."

Furious, Mup went to speak, but Fírinne intervened. Gently she took the woman's hand from Crow's arm. "Listen," she said.

The woman tried to pull away, but Fírinne held her in place. "No, please, listen. Queens and heirs mean nothing to me, you know that. I don't give a fig for the Speirling's rebellion. But earlier — just before we separated these children, just before we ripped their magic apart — I realized something. Watching those children dance the colour up out of the ground, I realized that I'd forgotten what it felt like to make magic."

The angry woman seemed to sag at Fírinne's words. Her eyes filled with tears. Around her the clann nodded or shook their heads. Each gesture was one of pain and of agreement — each meant the same thing: they'd all forgotten.

"But how is that even possible?" cried Mup. "I will never forget what it feels like to make magic. Never."

"Fear is a very effective weapon," said Fírinne softly. "And the queen uses it to its fullest capacity. Eventually we become anything she wants us to be, just so she'll leave us alone. But I don't want to live like that anymore. I don't want to go on forgetting that in my youth I danced colour up out of the ground and sang the stars ashiver, just for the joy of it."

"Me neither," whispered someone above Mup's head.

Fírinne nodded at them. "You all understand what it would mean for us if we use this level of outlaw magic. The queen will never leave us alone. We may never be able to run fast enough or far enough to escape her."

"We run all the time, anyway," said a woman.

The rest of the clann nodded.

"Let us do it," whispered Sealgaire.

"Hurrah!" cried Mup, clapping her hands. "Thank you! Thank you!"

"We'll make it quick," said Fírinne, suddenly brisk and enthusiastic. "We may be fools, but we're not suicidal. One great lifting of our voices to send the signal — then we run like the wind and hope her enforcers never catch us." She turned to the Speirling men. "What song is best suited to reach Speirling kind? Something courtly, I'll assume. A fugue? No! A madrigal!"

The men couldn't seem to believe their luck at the Clann'n Cheoil's willingness to fall in with their plan.

"See, Majesty," cried one of them to Mam,
"Simply by your presence,
How you motivate these peasants."

"Enough of that," snapped Fírinne. "Peasants, indeed! I should kick you back onto your knees, you brittle-spined toadies." She lifted her arms to gather her people into a circle. "Come on now, all together, like in the old days! Voices combined to send the signal—Clann'n Cheoil sing to form and carry the message Speirling, harmonize whatever tricky codes you have to let your people know where to meet us and to bring the heir's man. The music itself will hunt out the right ears to hear its meaning."

"The people who have my dad?" asked Mup.

Fírinne smiled and nodded. "And it will tell them a time and place to meet us with him. To anyone else it will just be a sound." She turned to Aunty, who was hovering, dim and fretful, by the caravans. "Duchess, will you sing?"

"Never," whispered Aunty. "And neither will Stella."

"I can't sing a note anyway," said Mam.

Fírinne grabbed her by her arms. "But, girl," she cried, "anyone can sing!" Her cheeks were flushed, her eyes bright, and Mup thought she was glowing suddenly, sparkling almost, with . . . was it happiness?

The corners of Mam's mouth lifted in a smile as Fírinne dragged her into the circle.

"Don't, Stella," said Aunty weakly. "You're . . . you're not used to it. You won't be able to control . . ."

"It's simple!" Fírinne told Mam. "Just let the music rise through you. Let it come down from the sky, let it come up from the ground. Open your heart. Close your eyes. Sing!" Fírinne extended her hand to Mup. "Come on, little one!"

"Crow too!" cried Mup, spinning in excitement to find her friend.

But Crow was striding away through the trees, already far from the caravans and the people—an angry, knotted-up storm cloud, alone in a forest of golden leaves.

"Leave him!" called the others as Mup ran to fetch him. "No time for his tantrums!"

Ignoring them, she kept running until she caught up with Crow deep in the trees.

"Hey!" she gasped. "Where are you going? The clann are going to help us!"

"Help you, you mean!" He spun to face her. "A year my dad has rotted in the queen's dungeons — a whole year! All that time, this lot did nothing to help him. Then you turn up!" He poked Mup in the shoulder. "You and your mam. Witch royalty! And suddenly it's 'Oh yes, Ma'am. Anything, Ma'am. Find your husband, Ma'am? In a trice, Ma'am!' "

"You're . . . you're forgetting to rhyme."

"Why should I rhyme? My whole life I've choked and stuttered and twisted my tongue! You mustn't talk, Crow. You must follow the rules, Crow. No dance magic. No singing. And now look!" He flung an arm to indicate the distant clann. They had already turned their backs, preparing to go ahead without him and Mup. "Suddenly they're doing choral magic. Choral magic! Risking it all to help the heir. To help the heir's man. Well, why not ever for Crow?" He slapped his chest. "Why not ever for Crow's dad?"

He was yelling into Mup's face, and the place where he had poked her shoulder felt sore. But there were tears in his round, dark eyes, and Mup felt more sorry for him than angry.

Crow covered his face with his hands. "I hate them. I hate everyone."

The sound of voices rose up from the road as

the people began to sing. It was a glorious sound, very strange and clear. Almost not like a sound at all, more like light moving through deep water, or new leaves opening across the face of a wood. Something physical and connected. Something that could travel the surface of the world. A message, designed for one person only to hear and understand.

Crow turned to it, like someone hungry, clearly wishing it was for him.

"We'll find your dad," said Mup. "I'll *make* them find him. We . . ."

But her friend had hopped backwards, his moment of openness gone as he spied someone coming up from the road. It was Sealgaire, running through the trees, Tipper and Badger hard on his heels. Crow cawed in anger and leapt from the ground, a bird in an instant, his glossy wings flapping.

"Come back here!" snapped Sealgaire as Crow landed high in a nearby tree.

Crow just cawed and clattered his beak.

"There's no time for tantrums!" yelled Sealgaire. "We must go before the queen's enforcers come!"

Crow just fluttered higher. Behind them, the song stopped. Sealgaire turned back to look at his people—they were already running for their caravans. The tornado-horses were whipping leaves up from the ground. High on his branch, Crow hopped defiantly from foot to foot.

"Crow!" bellowed Sealgaire. "I can't keep doing this for you! You're risking other people's lives!"

Some of the caravans began leaving. Sealgaire gripped Mup by the arm. "I'll leave you here!" he shouted to Crow. "I mean it this time!"

"I don't want to go with you anyway!" cawed Crow. "I hate you! I hate everyone!"

With a desperate cry, Sealgaire began dragging Mup back to the departing caravans.

"No!" she cried. "You can't leave him for the witches!"

Tipper circled them anxiously. "What's wrong with the birdy?"

Sealgaire would not look back. "He'll follow," he muttered. "He'll follow . . ."

Still striding forward, he glanced back. Crow remained stubbornly in place up his tree.

Mup yelled and dug her heels in. Badger growled and tried to pull her from Sealgaire's grip. But Sealgaire was much stronger than both of them, and he dragged them back to the caravan with no effort at all.

"Mam!" yelled Mup. "Make them wait for Crow!"

Mam paused at the door of Fírinne's *cáirín*, the wind from the tornado-horses whipping her hair about her face. Her dark eyes lifted to the angry raven clattering and hopping in the distant trees. For one moment Mup thought she would do something, but then Mam looked abruptly into the sky, gestured urgently to the others, and turned away.

"*Mam!*" screamed Mup.

But Mam had shut herself in. Then Mup too was inside a *cáirín*, flung up the steps by Sealgaire, with the dogs following quickly behind. The door slammed, and they were sealed into the crowded dimness.

The *cáirín* jerked to rattling life.

"Will Birdy fly after us?" whimpered Tipper as Mup pressed her face to the blue and yellow glass. The roadside trees were flashing past in a blur, Sealgaire's hair streaming back with the speed. Mup didn't think any bird would be capable of keeping up.

"They left him," she whispered. "They left poor Crow behind."

The More Important Child

By the time the band of cáiríní came to a halt, the sun had set and the woods had turned from gold to moonlit silver. Mup's rage, however, was still a burning coal in her chest. As soon as Sealgaire lifted the latch, she stormed down the steps and across to her mother, who was just descending into the narrow road. The clann were gathering around her, hushed and murmuring, their eyes roaming the shadow-filled trees. Mup shot through them like a little red bullet. "They left Crow!" she cried.

"Hush," said Aunty, grabbing her before she could get to Mam. "Hush. Listen!"

Gradually the stillness of their surroundings seeped through Mup's anger. It was so quiet. Even breathing seemed like a mistake.

Tipper came slinking to her left side, Badger to her right, and they all stood together, listening. They were at the edge of a village. The empty windows of the ornamented houses watched them. Each intricately painted door had a poster pinned to it, fluttering in the moonlight. The words were big, easy to read even from a distance:

By Order of the Queen:
DWELLINGS DEEMED UNLAWFUL.
INHABITANTS DISPENSED WITH.
REHABITATION PROHIBITED.

Who lived here? thought Mup. *Where have they gone?* She huddled deep into her jacket, chilled by the suspicion that wherever the former inhabitants had gone, it had been against their will, and whatever had happened to them, they would never return.

"Me scared," whispered Tipper.

"This was one of the first places to feel my sister's wrath," said Aunty. "The people here refused to paint over patterns which their grandmothers and great-grandmothers had designed. They could not believe the queen would end them, just because they wouldn't whitewash their houses."

136

Sealgaire came up softly beside Aunty.

"No one stood to fight for them, so they were taken away.

Their former homes stand as a warning to this very day."

Aunty looked sideways at him. "You chose this place as the rendezvous, didn't you? Thinking I'd forgotten."

"He left Crow behind!" said Mup. "He ran away and left him!"

Sealgaire glanced at her only briefly, then turned back to Aunty.

"I know what you want, Sealgaire," said Aunty, "and the answer is no. I've kept Stella safe from this her whole life. You'll not convince me to ruin her now by involving her in a losing battle. As soon as Daniel gets here, I'm taking him and her and these babies and we're all going home."

"But what about Crow?" insisted Mup.

Sealgaire, his eyes still locked with Aunty's, shook his head in disbelief.

"So, what Fírinne said about you is true.

The fate of your people means nothing to you.

I was convinced something bad had kept you from us . . .

That you must be dead or enchanted or worse.

But in truth you simply did not care.

You abandoned us to her."

"We were fools to think we could defeat my sister," said Aunty. "In the end I had my family to think about."

"Duchess, everyone you left behind had a family."

Aunty just jutted her chin. Desperately, Sealgaire's gaze slid to Mam, and Aunty's eyes narrowed. "Don't you dare try and drag Stella into this behind my back. This is not her fight."

"*Well, whose fight is it then?*" cried Sealgaire. For a moment his colours blazed fresh and clear in the murky light, then he deflated and they retreated to their faded state. He tilted his head, his black eyes very like Crow's as he stared into Aunty's stubborn face. "This has to be someone's fight, Duchess. *Someone* has to think we're important enough to stand up for."

Aunty simply tightened her lips and stayed silent until Sealgaire strode angrily away.

Mup took her glowing hand. "What did he mean?"

"It's not important."

"He left Crow behind, Aunty. He just left him in the woods."

"Oh, enough about that damned boy, Pearl. There's nothing we can do for him."

"Mam could make them go back for him, and—"

"Enough! He's not important. Do you understand? Only *you* are important. You and Stella and the baby!"

"But why am I more important than Crow?"

Aunty crouched, better to face Mup. She put her hand on Mup's cheek. "Because I love you, darling. Don't you know that? I love you. I'll always keep you safe."

Mup thought about this a moment. "But what if no one loved me? What if I was all alone, like Crow? Would I still be important enough to keep safe?"

Aunty dropped her hand from Mup's cheek. She sat back on her heels. "I . . . I never meant . . ."

Mam came striding over, all business. "It seems we'll be waiting a while for these people to show up with Daniel. Mup, you and Tipper should get some sleep. It's been a long day."

"I want to say hello to my daddy!" barked Tipper.

"Mam!" said Mup. "They left Crow behind in the woods. You have to make them go find him."

"Later," said Mam, distractedly looking out into the trees. "Off to bed now. Come on. I'll get you tucked up in Sealgaire's cáirín. By the time you wake up, your daddy will be here."

The cáirín's bed was in a pretty little alcove up near the ceiling. Filled with fat cushions, it was warm and cosy as a mouse's nest. Mup refused to get under the duvet and would only lie on top of the covers. She agreed to take off her shoes but held them tightly to her chest, fuming.

After Mam left them, Tipper and Badger climbed the wooden steps a few times to snuffle Mup's face, but there was no room for them in the bed, and eventually they lay down on the floor and fell asleep.

The village outside was very quiet. The moon shone bright through the stained-glass windows. Mup waited for Aunty to drift in on a moonbeam and check on her. She would give her a piece of her mind then. She'd *make* her talk about Crow. But Aunty did not check on her, and neither did Mam, and this made Mup feel strange and lonely and somehow invisible.

On the floor, Badger snored his old-man-dog snore and Tipper snored his little-baby-dog snore, and Mup was glad to hear them. She could not imagine how it might feel to be Crow, out there in the shifting silver and shadow world, knowing that no one would come if he called.

I suppose, she thought, *Crow is a very rude boy. Maybe if he was nicer, people would be more inclined to help him?*

But, in her heart, Mup knew that no matter how rudely she behaved, her family would never leave her alone in a dark forest. She also suspected that if her family *had* been the type of people to treat her like that, she might have grown up to be rather rude herself. She might have been downright nasty. *And then, she thought, people would be even more tempted to leave me behind.*

She rolled onto her side, watching the moonlight wink and shiver on all the many neat things in the *cáirín*. She thought of the empty village outside. Of its disappeared inhabitants that no one had come to help. She wondered if there were many children in the world like Crow. She had a horrible feeling that there might be. It hurt to think of how many of them might be out in the night, alone and lonely while she was curled up warm and safe, protected by the very same people who had left Crow behind. She clutched her shoes a little tighter and resolved to find him as soon as she could.

These thoughts were broken by a gentle pattering, like autumn leaves falling onto the roof. Mup sat up, listening. The pattering came faster, a strong gushing sound as if all the leaves in the world were pouring onto the roof of the *cáirín*. The light through the windows began to ripple with a torrent of falling shadows.

Mup put on her shoes, crept down the ladder, stepped over the sleeping dogs, and crept to the door.

Outside, all the trees seemed to be shedding the last of their autumn burden at once, and the night was arush with the sight and sound of falling leaves. The *clann* were gathered at their doors and in the road, looking about expectantly.

"The *Speirling* are coming," said Aunty, somewhere close at hand, and Mup peeped around the corner of the *cáirín* to see her and Sealgaire standing together in the dark. Sealgaire was looming over Aunty, his face all lit up with her ghost-light, while she stared up at him, her chin once again jutted in defiance.

"As soon as Daniel is here," she said, "Stella is going home. She's not going to sacrifice herself for your people."

> *"That is not your decision to make,*
> *The heir herself is the one to take—"*

"No! Stella has a nice life in the mundane world. She has the babies to keep her busy. She has her husband to keep her distracted. She doesn't *want* all this fighting and turmoil!"

"I haven't heard you *once* ask the heir what it is she wants to do!"

Aunty's reply was lost under the intense hiss and

patter of the leaves, which were falling thick as snow now. Mup crept closer, straining to hear. Sealgaire said something, and Aunty's eyes widened in fear. Sealgaire took something from his pocket—was it a necklace? Mup swiped the leaves from her vision, squinting as he held it up before Aunty, who shrank back. It *was* a necklace, a plaited leather cord from which dangled a heavy pendant in the shape of a glass bauble. Sealgaire thrust this towards Aunty. She flung her hands up in horror. There was a buzzing sound, and a crack of light. Then a noise like a kettle-whistle, and Aunty's ghost swirled and diminished as it was sucked upwards from the ground into the pendant, like water spinning into a drain.

Mup blinked. Aunty was gone. Only Sealgaire remained, standing in the flickering downpour of leaves, the pendant in his hand. Furtively, he put the necklace around his neck, tucked the glowing bauble beneath his shirt, and turned to go. Mup stepped out into his path, glaring, and he froze at the sight of her.

"I — I just want the chance to speak to the heir,
Without the duchess being there."

Mup went to speak, but a shout from the road sent them both spinning to look.

There were people descending from the tree-tops — floating downwards with the leaves. Haughty men and women, they were dressed in the courtly black clothing which identified them as part of the *Speirling Clann*. Their eyes scanned the road and trees and *cáiríní* as if expecting an attack. Mup's heart leapt at the sight of her dad suspended among them. Dazed-looking, he leaned against one of the sharp-faced men, his eyes half shut, his face tilted to the ground.

"Daddy!" cried Mup.

But even as she ran forward, a great wind rose up to disrupt the ordered downfall of leaves. A host of raggedy witches came stalking through the trees — their cold, pale, deadly faces hinting of tri-umph; their long, pale, deadly hands outstretched; their robes and hair like dark tempests around them.

"They've found us!" cried the *Speirling*. They ran, leaving Dad alone and dazed in the open ground between the caravans and the advancing witches.

"Get my children to safety!" cried Mam, striding through the knot of retreating *Speirling*, heading for her husband, who had slumped to his knees, apparently unaware of what was going on around him.

Mam lifted her hands, and lightning arced from

her fingertips, bringing the raggedy witches to a halt. Mup had never seen anything as wonderful as her mother at that moment—so blazing with ferocity, so full of crackling life and power, so clear and so focused that she shone. Everywhere she stepped, the forest glowed like a precious jewel.

She's so beautiful, thought Mup.

She ran to join her mother. As she ran, Mup felt her own arms rising, felt power tingle in her shoulders and along her spine. She clawed her fingers in imitation of Mam and held them out as a threat to the raggedy witches, who were already recovering from the shock of her mother's attack.

The queen's witches flexed their own hands. Webs of green fire laced their fingers. Some of them rose into the air, separating so that Mam had to divide her attention here and there as she countered their witch-fire with her own.

"Daniel!" yelled Mam, firing and striding forward still. "Come to me!"

The others—*Clann'n Cheoil* and *Speirling*—had clustered together by the caravans, huddled and afraid. But seeing Mam fighting the raggedy witches alone seemed to do something to them. One of the men suddenly ran to her side, fire gushing from his palms. After a tiny hesitation, a woman ran to join him. Then another, and soon all of the Clann'n Cheoil and some of the Speirling were rushing forward.

The raggedy witches seemed everywhere now, emerging from the trees. Lightning blasted and fire roared. Great fountains of leaves flew in blinding showers. Men and women fell, some screaming, some horribly still. A raggedy witch plummeted from the treetops like a dark comet, to land in an explosion of leaves close by. At the heart of the chaos, Dad looked up as Mam called his name again. He squinted at her but made no effort to rise from his knees. The raggedy witches were all about him.

"Dad!" yelled Mup, still running. "Get up!" Sparks and glitter fizzed and spat at her fingertips, useless as a sparkler at Halloween.

Behind her Tipper barked.

Mam—still striding towards Dad—yelled to the people behind her. "Get my children out of here!"

Lightning gouged the ground at Mup's feet. Earth and leaves coughed upwards, obscuring her view. Suddenly, strong hands gripped her shoulders and she was yanked backwards and up. Someone was running with her in their arms, her face and hands trapped against their chest. She couldn't move and she couldn't see! Tipper barked angrily, and Badger too, over and over again.

Terrified, Mup pushed against the person's chest. There was a fierce, *channelling* sensation. Something like pain convulsed her hands. The person carrying her screamed, and she was blasted from their arms, the two of them thrust in opposite directions.

Mup fell. Her head hit something, a stone maybe, and there were stars.

Someone strode past her. A woman. Mup realized to her vague dismay that it was a raggedy witch. The ends of the woman's dark cloak trailed Mup's face as she crossed, unheeding of Mup's limp body, to the huddled man, who only moments before had been carrying Mup in his arms.

She doesn't see me, Mup thought dimly, *because I'm buried in these leaves.*

The witch stooped to look closely at the man. The silver streak in her hair glimmered in the firelight, and Mup recognized her as the witch who had tried to steal Mam away the night Aunty died. Behind her, trees were burning, rebels ran and screamed. The witch showed no reaction to these awful things. She spoke to the man on the ground. "Sealgaire."

He lifted his head. "Magda."

The witch straightened as Sealgaire tried to rise, and watched expressionlessly as he fell back into the leaves with a groan. "Is the child gone from you?" she asked.

"Gone . . ." gasped Sealgaire. "Gone . . . into the forest."

"He was never to bother me. That was the deal. Yet he is increasingly unlawful."

"I'm . . . I'm sorry . . . Please don't hurt him . . ."

The witch sighed. With another groan of pain, Sealgaire struggled to his hands and knees and began to crawl from her. She tilted her head, as if considering what to do with him, then sighed again.

"You may leave," she said, already turning away. "But consider our agreement ended, brother. Pray the boy never crosses my path."

Sealgaire crawled from Mup's view. Through the growing blossoms of darkness which now crowded her vision, Mup saw *cáiríní* on fire, trees splintered and smouldering.

The rebels and her mother fought on, but even as they tried to save him, her dad, limp as a rag, was lifted into a cloud of raggedy witches and carried skyward on a pillar of smoke. *Dad* . . . Weakly stretching her hand from the leaves, Mup tried to shoot a flame that might save him. Sparks sputtered and died at her fingertips.

Mup's hand fell back into the leaves, no longer under her control. She could only lie there and watch helplessly as the witches carried Dad away.

Something blocked her vision. It was Sealgaire, his face bloody and creased with pain.

Help Dad, she thought. *Help him.*

Sealgaire brushed the leaves from her. She felt herself being lifted again and slung across his shoulder. He staggered away with her in his arms as lightning and noise shook the ground behind them.

Mup thought, *No, stop,* but the darkness won and she knew no more.

Wanted

Mup woke to a rattling and a bumping and to something warm and sloppy slathering her face.

"Ugh," she moaned, opening her eyes. "Stop."

She was greeted with an extreme close-up of Tipper's anxious face. "Am you alive?" he whispered. "You has blood on your head and you's been asleep so long the sun has comed up."

He was nudged aside so that Badger could snuffle her up and down. Apparently satisfied that she wasn't dead, both dogs went back to earnestly licking her face.

"Ugh!" Mup pushed them aside. "Stop! I'm already soaked!"

The world lurched—a massive, clattering jolt— and girl and dogs had to hold on as the floor beneath them tilted alarmingly.

Mup realized they were inside Sealgaire's *cáirín*, and they seemed to be travelling at enormous speed. Little tin pots and fragile, painted teacups tinkled and smashed from the shelves. Small paintings shivered and fell. Ashes puffed from the rattling stove. It was as though the whole lovely home was shaking itself apart.

Unable to gain her feet on the jolting floor, Mup crawled to the front of the *cáirín* and opened the door. It slammed back on its hinges, admitting a ferocious wind which snatched Mup's hair and sent curtains and books and bedclothes flying about the interior.

"Sealgaire!" yelled Mup above the noise. "What's happening?"

The man was hunched in the driver's seat, one arm wrapped tight around his body, the reins clenched in his free hand. Still on her hands and knees, Mup clutched the door frame, terrified at the sudden understanding that they were rocketing along above the trees, nothing but air and dislodged leaves between them and the distant ground.

"We're flying!" she yelled.

Her voice roused Sealgaire, who until then had not noticed her. He lifted his head, and Mup had just enough time to see how ashen his face was, how creased in pain, before he toppled from the porch and, to Mup's horror, fell to the ground below.

As soon as Sealgaire released the reins, the tornado-horses began to buck. The *cáirín* began swinging from side to side, and all its contents — dogs and lamps and dishes and bedclothes — hurled about within.

Mup clung on for dear life. The loose reins slapped and flapped in the wind, tantalizingly just outside her grasp. Gathering her courage, Mup grabbed for them. The *cáirín* fell away from under her, so that for a moment she was suspended in the air. Then she slammed back down onto the porch, the breath driven from her even as she hauled back on the reins.

"Whoa, horsies!" she gasped. "Whoa!"

It seemed a ridiculous thing to say to two tethered tornados spinning thirty feet above the ground. But the moment she said it, the horses tamed, the vehicle straightened, and Mup found herself in command of a flying *cáirín*.

The golden trees sped past below, the clear sky streamed above, and for a moment Mup was afraid to do anything to disrupt their steady forward motion. But she couldn't just keep going on and on to the horizon. Gently, she tugged the left-hand rein. The horses veered, the cáirín turned, and Mup found herself heading back the way they'd come.

Glass tinkled behind her as the dogs came creeping onto the porch to look over the edge. Tipper's ears and tongue flew back in the breeze. Badger turned uncertain eyes to her.

"Keep an eye out for Sealgaire," she yelled. "He fell out. I think he's hurt!"

How am I ever going to land? she thought.

"There he is!" barked Tipper. "Down there in the road!"

Sure enough, Sealgaire's body lay where it must have landed, in a crater of leaves far below. Already they were leaving him behind, the horses travelling steadfastly onwards. Mup carefully turned them again, and soon they were circling the sky above Sealgaire's motionless body.

"What do I do?" she yelled. "We can't keep going round and round like this."

"Down, horsies!" barked Tipper. "Down!"

The horses ignored him.

Impatient now, Mup slapped the reins. "DOWN!" she yelled.

To her consternation, instead of circling gently down as she had hoped, the horses reared in anger.

They neighed furiously, which sounded like a stormy gust of wind, and just like that, they were gone.

"Ohhhhhh noooooooooo!" howled Tipper as, horseless, they plummeted downwards.

The *cáirín* tilted on one end as it fell, its front door facing the dawn-tinted clouds. Mup and Badger and Tipper clung to the porch while all the lovely bits and pieces of Sealgaire's once tidy home spilled from the door.

Snap, bang, splinter—the *cáirín* crashed through the delicate interlacing of branches below.

Then—*whoosh*—it broke through the canopy of airy trees to smack, back-end first, into the soft ground, where it stood, its wheels spinning gently, its door facing the sky like the open mouth of a beautifully painted well. Mup fell all the way down to the bottom of this well. She slammed into the little bed alcove, which was still lined with pillows and cushions and duvets.

All the contents of the *cáirín* that had been flung up into the air paused overhead—as if surveying the blue sky and trees, trying to decide where they wanted to be. Then they tumbled back down, burying Mup in a clattering stream of books and bottles and curtains and plates until there was no sign of her at all.

For a long time, nothing moved. Then the silence was broken by a clink and a shuffle and the rattle of things being shoved aside as Mup struggled out from the heap of duvets that had protected her from the avalanche.

"Tipper?" she yelled. "Badger? Is everyone OK?"

She was part of a jumbled heap of horribly tangled, broken things. The door was a square of blue sky overhead, well out of her reach. Luckily the walls of the *cáirín* were lined with many shelves, which Mup found she could climb like a ladder.

As she clambered her way up, Tipper's face popped into the rectangle of sky which was the front door. Badger appeared at his side. The older dog woofed once, then disappeared again. Mup heard his nails scrabbling the boards of the *cáirín* as he scrambled down the outside wall and then the shush of his feet in the leaves as he ran away.

"Are you OK, Tipper?" panted Mup, still climbing upwards.

Tipper whined anxiously. "I think something is wrong with the birdy-man. He can't stand up."

"Just wait for me," called Mup. "Wait!"

But Tipper had already gone. She heard him leap

from the porch as he followed Badger. Then she was up in the fresh air, pulling herself from the interior of the *cáirín* like a mole exiting a hole in the ground. She stood and surveyed the damage.

What a sad sight. Sealgaire's lovely home was ruined.

Crow's home, Mup reminded herself. Sealgaire was only minding it for him.

Jumping from the splintered porch, she ran to where the dogs were sniffing Sealgaire's body.

"Come away from him!" she yelled. "He's a bad man! He was talking to a raggedy witch!"

She yanked Tipper away by his scruff, making him yelp, and dragged him a safe distance from the man who lay face down and motionless in the leaves.

Badger remained, tentatively sniffing Sealgaire's hands and the tangled sprawl of his long hair.

Suddenly Sealgaire began to groan and move.

"Come away, Badger!" cried Mup.

Badger retreated, whining, and they watched as Sealgaire tried to lift himself to his knees.

Mup's anger faded a little as he flopped back onto the ground.

"Tipper," she whispered, gently pushing her little brother to sit beside Badger. "Stay."

She crept forward as Sealgaire once again tried to rise.

He was groaning as if in terrible pain. Against her wishes, Mup felt her sympathy for him grow. Nevertheless, when Sealgaire finally managed to roll onto his side, she crouched and raised her hands in warning, her fingers alive with sparks.

Sealgaire just lay curled around himself, watching her through eyes that were barely open. Mup could see a great scorched hole in his coat and shirt; the skin beneath looked blackened and burned.

She straightened, and the sparks which had been dancing on her fingertips died away.

"The birdy-man is sore," whispered Tipper, creeping to her side.

Mup pushed him behind her. "Stay with Badger, Tip."

Motionless, Sealgaire watched as she sat in the leaves before him.

"Are you all right?" she asked, eyeing his discoloured flesh.

Sealgaire took a shivering breath. "No."

She lifted the burned edges of his coat and he closed his eyes, his teeth bared in pain. Burned clearly into his flesh were two handprints. They were the size and shape of Mup's hands. She dropped Sealgaire's coat back over them, not wanting to see them anymore. Not wanting to think about them.

"Wh-why did you carry me off?"

He looked up at her through the net of his hair. "We were losing the fight . . . didn't want her witches to get you."

"You should have trusted Mam to win, Sealgaire. She could have protected me and Tip. Now the queen's witches have Dad, and instead of me being there to help Mam, she'll have to worry about finding him and us!"

"Listen." Sealgaire turned his head painfully and indicated a narrow path which meandered away into the woods. "There . . . there is a town close to here . . . I . . ."

He closed his eyes, forcing himself to concentrate on his words.

> *There is a town close to here,*
> *Food and shelter you'll find there.*
> *Follow . . . follow the rules . . . live quietly,*
> *Perhaps your mother . . . will come for thee.*

This lesson I could not teach Crow,

This wisdom he refused to know."

"You're working with the raggedy witches," said Mup. "I saw you talking to one of them."

"No, no . . . you misunderstand . . . Crow . . . That was Crow's . . ."

"You left Crow in the woods!" cried Mup, her anger rising again despite her sympathy. "He's just a little kid, but you ran off and left him out there on his own."

"In times like these, one has to know,

Whom to protect, whom to let go."

"You only rescued me because you want my mam to do things for you," said Mup. "That's the only reason. If Mam hadn't been who she is, you'd have left me too."

A sighing whisper rose up from the collar of Sealgaire's shirt. Cautiously, one sparking hand raised in warning, Mup shifted the man's straggled hair and uncovered the small, pulsing globe of the necklace. Its catch was broken, and she easily pulled it free from under him.

The pendant hummed in her hand. Aunty's voice—the faintest whisper, as if only in Mup's mind—spoke to the man who lay before her: "History shall judge you and me, Sealgaire, by how we abandoned the weakest among us. By how we failed to help those who had nothing to offer in return."

Sealgaire muttered:

"Save your breath and spare my ears,

I've tried my best here all these years."

"And when push came to shove, you abandoned one who needed you. We're not so different, you and me."

Sealgaire squeezed his eyes shut again and turned his face away as if in shame.

"Tell me how to get to the queen's castle," Mup asked him.

He gasped in horror and shook his head.

"Tell me!" insisted Mup. "I'll go there myself and get my dad and whoever else the witches have taken. I'll tell the queen that my mam doesn't want her stinking crown."

"Little girl, both brave and true,

I would not inflict the queen on you."

Mup leapt to her feet. She tied the pendant around her neck. "Fine!" she said. "I'll go to your stupid town and make someone else tell me the way!"

She marched off down the path.

Tipper and Badger followed uncertainly in her wake. Aunty whispered and sighed around her neck. Mup marched on, teeth gritted, fists clenched, her bright green wellies churning up the leaves, until Sealgaire and his ruined home were out of sight. Then she slowed, and faltered, and stopped in the road, her head down, panting.

Sealgaire had abandoned Crow. He had put Aunty in a necklace.

But Sealgaire was also hurt. He was also all alone. Mup couldn't leave him.

She sighed. She turned around and walked back.

Sealgaire did not move as she crouched down beside him, but he cracked a glittering eye.

"Can you walk?" she asked.

He shook his head.

"Change into a raven, then. I can carry you to help. There's sure to be a doctor in the town."

Sealgaire surprised her by smiling. Tears leaked from his eyes as he closed them again. "My time is up."

"What do you mean?"

Sealgaire shifted his hand slightly in the leaves, and Mup, not wanting him to be lonely, took it in her own.

"I am sorry for whatever hurt I have inflicted," he whispered, "and for any good I failed to do in my life." He gently squeezed her fingers. "In truth, I only ever wanted . . ."

Sealgaire's hand relaxed suddenly, as if he'd fallen asleep, and he stopped talking.

"Sealgaire?" said Mup. She shook his shoulder. "Sealgaire?"

Sealgaire did not move, and Mup sat back — realizing that he had been much more badly hurt than she had first understood. She sat like that for a long time, holding Sealgaire's hand, hoping that he might speak or move again. When she was certain he wouldn't, she and the dogs gently covered him in a blanket of bright autumn leaves. Then, reluctantly and with many a backward look, they left his body and took the meandering path to the nearest town.

They walked for hours, following the narrow path and seeing no one. Mup kept looking straight ahead, trying not to think too deeply about what had just happened. Tipper kept looking back the way they'd come.

"Mup?" he whimpered. "Are you sure the birdy-man will be OK under the leafs?"

"Yes, Tipper. Don't worry about him."

"But will he not be cold? Will he not be lonely?"

Mup hesitated. She had been hoping Aunty might come up with a way to explain things to Tipper. Mup didn't think she had the right words to do so without frightening her little brother, or upsetting him. But Aunty just grumbled and sighed softly in the pendant round Mup's neck, as if preoccupied with her own thoughts.

"Mup?" Tipper nudged her hand with his small wet nose. "Mup, is . . . is the birdy-man dead?"

Mup stopped walking, her eyes suddenly full of tears.

Tipper wagged his tail hopefully. "Has he turned into a ghost like Aunty?" he asked. "Is he all floaty and sparkly and happy now?"

Floaty and sparkly and happy. Is that how Tipper saw Aunty's ghost? Mup tried to see things from Tipper's very-small-person's point of view, and she supposed that that might be how things seemed to him. She straightened her back and dashed the tears from her eyes. She smiled for Tipper.

"Yes," she said. "Yes, Tipper. Sealgaire is a ghost now, just like Aunty. He's sparkly and floaty and . . ."

"Happy?" asked Tipper, his tail wagging faster.

"Yes," said Mup. "Happy."

"OK!" barked Tipper, his big grin back on his

golden face. "Yay!" He bounded off to pass this news on to Badger, who was gazing up at a weathered road sign some way off down the path.

"Badger!" barked Tipper. "Sealgaire is dead and he's very happy now!"

Mup closed her hand around the pendant. *Is that true, Aunty?* she asked. *Is Sealgaire happy now?*

But Aunty just swirled and sighed and grumbled. *"Memories, memories."*

Mup wondered what it was that Sealgaire had been going to tell her back there before he had died. What it was he had wanted. Perhaps he had only ever wanted a nice quiet life — just like Aunty had had. Perhaps he had only ever wanted to get up and go to work, and come home and watch telly, and help his kids with their homework. Perhaps that would have been enough for him.

More than enough.

Mup thought of what Sealgaire had told Aunty — how he had waited for years, thinking she'd come back and help them and their people. All that time, Aunty had been with Mup and Mam and Tipper, knitting and smiling and living the happy life Sealgaire longed for.

Mup wondered if it was OK to do that. Have a warm and comfy life when other people didn't?

She couldn't see how living a nice life would be a bad thing—after all, Mup was sure that given half a chance, Fírinne and Sealgaire would choose just such a life for themselves.

But they hadn't, thought Mup. She remembered Sealgaire asking what would happen if everyone chose to run away. Who would remain to right the wrongs? She thought of him tilting his head, his black eyes very like Crow's as he stared into Aunty's face. "This has to be someone's fight," he'd said. "Someone has to think we're important enough to stand up for."

What am I going to do? thought Mup as she made her way to the dogs. I don't know where Mam is. I don't know the way to the queen's castle or if Dad really is there. Even if I find someone to ask directions, I don't know if I'd trust anyone here to really show me the way.

"What are you looking at?" she asked, gazing up at the fluttering posters on the road sign which so intrigued the dogs. Her grip tightened on the pendant as she recognized what they were.

"It's the birdy-men," panted Tipper. "And the cat-ladies. All in a row. Aren't they pretty drawings, Mup?"

"Yes, they are," said Mup, reaching to unpin the fragile paper from the wood. "Very pretty."

They were indeed beautiful drawings, each one a portrait of a man or a woman. Shuffling from one page to the next, Mup recognized Fírinne and Sealgaire and all the other members of the *Clann'n Cheoil*, in both their animal and human forms.

Printed clearly across the top of each grim portrait were the words:

By Order of Her Majesty the Queen:

WANTED ALIVE OR DEAD

REWARD PAYABLE ON
DELIVERY TO THE CASTLE.

Mup rolled up the posters and slipped them into her backpack. She looked down the road to where threads of smoke were just visible rising above the trees—the chimney smoke of a village, perhaps. They must be very near to the town where Sealgaire had hoped she'd hide and wait for rescue.

Straightening her hat, Mup set off once again.

Tipper and Badger trotted after her. "Where am we going, Mup?"

"To town."

"Will Mammy be there?"

"Nope."

"Will there be sandwiches?"

"I don't think so."

"What will we do in town?"

"Well, Tipper, I very much hope we'll get ourselves arrested."

A Determined Prisoner

"Oh no, no, no, no, no," said the first police officer, shaking her heavy head. "No."

"I absolutely agree," said the second officer. "One hundred per cent."

"But I really very much insist," said Mup. She once again waved the wanted posters. "Please be so kind as to arrest me."

"No," said the first police officer, and she put her large hands over her ears and closed her round eyes. "What I can't see can't hurt me," she said.

"Why, this is just ridiculous," muttered Mup.

When she and the dogs had first come into the tiny, marshy town, the two police officers—standing on the porch of their mossy little riverside shack— had smiled and nodded and fondly patted the dogs' heads. But as soon as Mup had mentioned the queen's castle and the possibility of being transported there, things had changed. Both officers had turned their backs, faced the wall of the porch, and had done their best to pretend she wasn't there.

"I am the *heir's daughter*," cried Mup. "I absolutely insist that you arrest me and take me to the castle so I can talk to my grandmother!"

At these words, the second officer shrieked and leapt into the water.

"I know you can hear me!" yelled Mup to the top of his bald head, which was just visible among the lily pads.

The other officer opened one reluctant eye. "Please don't make us go to the queen. We lead a quiet life here. No one bothers with us. Why would we want to change that?"

Mup patted her arm. "I really am sorry," she said, genuinely meaning it. "But people's houses are burning to the ground and people are dying, and there are kids who are left out in the dark all on their own. I'd very much like to try and change that."

The police officer seated Mup and the dogs quite comfortably on a large pile of rugs in the corner of a very large cage in the centre of a raft, which she then proceeded to guide downstream with the aid of a pole.

"It's not fair," she muttered. "Expecting an officer of the law to risk life and limb transporting a convict into the very arms of the queen." She shuddered. "Thought I'd go my whole life without having to lay eyes on one of them awful grim-faced witches of hers, and now look at me . . ."

"You've never seen a raggedy witch?" asked Mup.

"Why would I? I told you, we lead a quiet, obedient life! Why would they bother us any?"

"Well . . . what if one of your menfolk forgets to rhyme?"

"Forgets to rhyme? What do you take us for in Marsh Bottom? Bloomin' *rebels*? Bloomin' *storytellers* and *artists* and *historians*?" The officer spat into the water. "Rhyme! Only troublemakers have to rhyme, and they bring that on themselves. *Them that speaks no evil can speak as they please*," she said, as if quoting a well-known saying. "You won't find no one in Marsh Bottom as will speak out foul against the queen."

"No matter what she does to other people," said Mup quietly, beginning to understand.

The officer just looked at her from the corner of

her big golden eyes and went on poling with the current.

Eventually, the fields on either side of the river gave way to cottages, and soon the countryside retreated in favour of another small riverside town. Little children ran along the banks, pointing at the cage and shouting.

A thoughtful look grew on the officer's face, and she angled the pole against the river in such a way as to bring the raft closer to the banks. "Tell your constabulary to meet me at the jetty," she shouted to the children. "I have some cargo for them to transfer downstream."

The children ran off, and the officer guided the raft in against the wall of a little stone harbour. Badger and Tipper sniffed the air curiously, and Mup peered up through the bars of the cage. Everything was alive with reflected light. There was no sound but the *slap, slap* of the water and the distant shouts of the children as they ran to deliver their message. There was the scent of flowers, the smell of fresh-baked bread.

Everything seems so normal, Mup thought. *Everyone seems so happy.*

"We'll keep this nice and simple," said the officer,

hanging the keys to the cage on the steering pole and drawing a notebook from the pocket of her voluminous coat. She licked the end of her pencil and wrote in large purple letters:

By Order of the Queen:

CONVICTS.
FOR TRANSPORT TO THE CASTLE.

"There we go," she said, attaching the note to the outside of the padlocked cage. "No longer my problem." And she plopped into the water without so much as a *goodbye* or *see you later*, and left Mup and the dogs to their fate.

Mup crept forward to touch the fluttering paper.

Everyone seems so happy, she thought again. *But under it all, they're terrified.*

"Oh no, no, no, no," said the officers of the new town. "No way are we going to the castle. No way. No how."

"But they can't stay here!" cried the people of the town. "What if the queen sends her witches for them! Who knows what laws we might be breaking just standing here and talking about it! They'd sniff out all our failings. We'd be thrown in jail in the blink of an eye." With that, the people bundled the officers onto the raft and shoved it out from the wall, sending them spinning downstream before they could even think of a reply.

"This is what comes of discontent," grumbled one of the new officers, sulkily eyeing Mup and the dogs. "This is what comes of people not doing what the queen wants. Rebels. Pah! They're never bloomin' happy."

"Some might say they have no cause to be happy," murmured her companion quietly, steering the raft. "What with houses burned and people chucked in jail just for talking a bit different and dressing a bit different and singing songs the queen don't like and such. Personally, I don't see any harm in being a bit different, me. *Variety is the spice of life*, my old nan used to say."

"Yes, and we all know what happened to your old nan, don't we?" snapped his friend.

"What happened to her?" asked Mup from her nest of rugs inside the cage. "Was she arrested? Perhaps she's in the castle! I can look for her while I'm there, if you like?"

The officer seemed startled by this suggestion. "Would . . . would you do that?" he asked.

"Of course I would," said Mup. "If your nan is in trouble, why wouldn't I try to help her?"

In the pendant around Mup's neck, Aunty began to stir and mutter—"*Memories, memories.*" To Mup's ears, the water lapping under the raft and the reeds rustling on the banks of the river seemed to murmur in reply.

The guards abandoned them in a strange, dark harbour in the dead of the night. It took a very long time for anyone to come down the harbour steps. Though many people gathered on the harbour wall to murmur and watch, no one wanted to take them to the queen, it seemed. Everyone was desperate to pass the responsibility on to someone else.

Eventually a tall, thin woman led a nervous man down the steps. The woman was older than any of the previous officers, and she peered curiously in at Mup as she climbed on board the raft. "Are you part of the revolution?" she whispered.

"Hush," said her companion. "Not when we're still so close to shore." He sighed as he handed her the steering pole and shoved the keys into his pocket. "Let's get this over with."

The people of the town, silent and guarded, watched as the officers pushed the raft out onto the river. They were nothing but dark shapes cut from the starry sky. Mup knelt to peer through the bars as they and their moonlit town drifted from view.

The pendant around her neck was quiet. If Mup listened carefully, she could hear a faint snoring coming from it. Aunty had gone asleep. On the rugs, Tipper had settled down by Badger's side, and both dogs had closed their eyes.

The female guard kept gazing out into the reeds as she steered the raft, and she spoke very quietly, barely moving her lips. "I hear there's been a return to combined magics among the rebels. Combined magics such as haven't happened since the queen's sister left the borough."

Mup crept to the door of the cage. "Do you mean like . . . choral magic?" she asked. "And dance magic?"

Both guards looked sharply at her. "Yes," they whispered. "Is it true?"

"Well, yes," said Mup. "I've seen it. I've *danced* it."

The male officer leapt to his feet and fled to the other end of the raft, as if too frightened to even hear the words. The woman regarded Mup with wide eyes. "How wonderful," she breathed.

"Perhaps . . ." whispered the man, out of sight at the head of the raft, "perhaps a better time might be coming."

"But if you want change so badly, why wait for someone else to get it for you?" asked Mup. "Surely if you work together . . ."

"Easier said than done," murmured the woman. "Who'd be the first to speak out, when speaking out means being dragged away? Who'd be mad enough to stand for change, when odds are, you'll stand alone?"

"And die alone," muttered her companion. "With none but the enforcers to know where or when."

The pendant at Mup's neck snorted, as if this statement had woken it. Once again it began to whisper. Mup could not understand the words, but once again the trees and the riverbank and the water all sighed and murmured in reply. It felt like something old was stirring all around them: memories, perhaps; ghosts.

Mup shivered. "Can you hear that?" she asked.

But the guards shook their heads.

The raft drifted into a tunnel of overhanging willows. Moonlight filtered through the leaves and shone up from the dark water, rippling the trunks like an undersea cave. The sequins on Mup's tutu spangled the darkness with light. Aunty once again grew silent. The whispers fell behind.

Soon the guards fell asleep, and Mup was surrounded by snores. She was the only passenger awake on the gently drifting craft. She had to admit she felt scared and kind of lonely, even with the dogs on either side of her and the two grown-ups guarding her.

Those guards won't protect me, she thought. *When the witches come, those guards will run away and leave me and Tipper and Badger to face them on our own.*

As if Mup's thoughts had summoned it, a dark shape crossed the moon. A shadow blotted the dappled light, and something landed in the trees above.

Mup sat up.

The witches were here. They'd come for her.

She went to wake the dogs, meaning for them all to stand together. But something made her stop. Looking down at Tipper's peacefully sleeping face and Badger's old grey muzzle, Mup thought, *no,* and she rose quietly instead, and stepped off the rugs alone.

I'll go peacefully, she thought. *Let the witches take just me.*

Badger and Tipper could drift onwards, unharmed. Mup would face her grandmother on her own.

"I see you," she whispered as a big, dark shape worked its way down through the branches towards her. "I'm not afraid."

The black shape swooped from the branches and landed in the darkness at the back of the raft, close to the feet of a sleeping guard. Mup pressed her face to the bars, trying to see as the shape fluttered and hopped. There was a clink of metal, the rustle of stiff cloth or outstretched wings.

A breeze buffeted Mup's face as the shape launched itself, flapping, to the bars above her. A great, round, dark eye looked down. The keys to the cage dangled from a gleaming beak.

"Not afraid?" whispered Crow.

"Are you mad?

What if I'd been someone bad?"

They greeted each other in a storm of happy whispers and clackings of beak. Mup shoved her arms up through the bars and hugged Crow's feathered neck so hard that he said *"ACK"* and begged to be released before he choked.

"With just a hopping and a click," he whispered, swinging upside down from the cage and expertly fitting the keys into the padlock.

"Crow will get you out of this!"

Mup put her hand on the lock. "Wait, Crow," she said. "I have a different plan."

A yawn behind her made both of them freeze.

Mup groaned as two big brown eyes opened in the dark.

"Birdy!" exclaimed Tipper. "Birdy is back!"

"Shh," hissed Mup urgently. "Don't wake the guards."

Tipper scrambled forward, all paws and excitement. "Mup was very angry you was left behind," he whispered up at Crow. "She shouted and made horrible faces at everyone."

Mup blushed.

Crow eyed her curiously and clacked his beak.

Tipper rushed on. "She scolded the birdy-man, very much, all the time. But he wouldn't go back for you and then the caravan falled—BANG!—out of the sky and the birdy-man is dead, but it's OK because Mup says he's a ghost and happy and—"

Mup put her hand on Tipper's muzzle. "Tipper," she said. "Stop talking."

Crow just tilted his head and looked at her and blinked his round black eyes. It was hard to judge his emotions—especially when he was in his bird form. Mup wasn't sure he understood.

"Tipper is talking about Sealgaire, Crow. The witches came and Sealgaire got hurt trying to save me from them. We . . . we had to bury him under the leaves."

Crow chattered his beak very softly, and Mup thought that maybe he couldn't find any words to express how sad he felt about his friend.

"We're all jail-birds here, Crow," she whispered. "You don't need to rhyme anymore."

"Sealgaire rescued you from the witches? He . . . he fought the witches for you?"

"Oh, Crow," whispered Mup, suddenly understanding. Sealgaire had left Crow in the woods—he had left him at the mercy of the witches—only to lay down his life that very same night for Mup. "Crow. I'm so sorry . . ."

Crow didn't say anything. He just unlocked the cage door, hopped up onto Mup's knee, lay his head on her shoulder, and was very quiet for a long time.

* * *

When the guards woke in the morning, with the sun just kissing the reeds on the riverbank and the little birds starting to sing in the misty trees, they were more than startled to find the keys hanging from the securely locked padlock and a large, young raven fast asleep with the others on the rugs: one more convict determined to be taken to the queen.

Disreputable Changes

"Come on, little brother," Crow insisted. "Try harder!"

"But I *ams* trying!" said Tipper, and he once again screwed up his face in concentration and tensed his body.

"I don't like this," muttered the male guard. "I don't like this at all."

"Ah, who cares what you like?" said Crow, and he blew a raspberry through the bars of the cage before turning back to Tipper.

From her perch on the rugs, Mup watched her brother very carefully for any sign of him turning back into a boy, but all that happened was that Tipper went a little red in the face and farted.

He and Mup fell around the place laughing. Crow just sighed.

The two guards shook their heads anxiously. "I wish you wouldn't practise forbidden magics on board the raft," said the female guard. "What if someone sees you?"

"We're already *prisoners!*" said Mup. "What trouble could you possibly get into?"

"Besides, there's nothing forbidden about changing." Crow sniffed. "Everyone changes." And as if to demonstrate, he changed from boy to raven and back again in dizzyingly quick succession.

"You know what I *mean!*" hissed the woman. "Men is always ravens, women is always cats—nice and neat and respectable. There's nothing respectable about . . ." She waved a hand at Tipper as if hardly knowing what to call him. "I mean, whoever heard of a person turning into a *dog?*"

"Weren't always just cats and ravens," said the male guard. "Was a time folks became whatever they chose whenever they chose. Birds, cats, dogs, fishes . . . whatever best suited a body's nature and mood." He eyed Tipper uncertainly. "Though I never heard of a body not being able to change back. Not even in the old days. What happened to you, boy? Did you get a fright?"

"Perhaps the wind changed, and he stuck like that?" said the woman.

"Possible . . ."

"Perhaps he just enjoys being a puppy," said Mup, not liking how uncomfortable this conversation was making Tipper. "Perhaps he just doesn't *want* to change back." Tipper trotted over to her and licked her face. Mup scratched his ears. "Is that it, Tipper?" she asked. "Are you just having lots of fun being a puppy?"

He whispered in her ear, as if ashamed for the others to hear. "I likes being able to run instead of being carried," he said. "I likes making my wee-wee in a bush."

"You know you can do those things as a boy too, Tipper, right? You just have to be patient and learn."

He looked up at her uncertainly. "Don't you like me when I is a puppy, Mup?"

"Oh, Tipper! I *love* you, no matter what you are." She glared pointedly at the officers. "Not everyone has to be the same," she said. "No matter what the queen says."

The officers looked like they might die of consternation at that. But Tipper barked in relief and chased his tail for a minute, then flopped onto his back, panting.

"WOOF!" he said in his little-boy voice, and even Crow had to smile.

He ran his hand through Tipper's golden fur. "Is he that colour as a boy?" he asked.

"Yes. Tipper is a chubby little fair-haired baby, aren't you, Tipper?"

"No!" barked Tipper. "I'm a puppy!"

Crow eyed Mup's skin and hair. "You're not alike," he said.

Mup smiled. "I take after Dad. Tipper is more like Mam. She says me and Tip are beautiful in different ways."

"Your father is a Norseman?" asked Crow curiously.

"A Norseman? Like . . . a Viking?"

"Yes. People from the North have the same dark hair and skin as you."

Mup laughed—imagining her dad in a Viking helmet. "Where I'm from Vikings are blond!"

"Oh." Crow seemed disappointed. "Your dad's not a Norseman, then?"

"My dad's from Ireland, like me." Mup smiled. "But his mam and dad are from Nigeria."

Thinking of her dad made Mup worry again— where he might be, what might be happening to him—and she twisted to look the way they were travelling. Ahead of them, the river wound through endless trees, their leaves drifting down to coat the slow-moving water.

"Your father must make a handsome raven," said Crow. "Very sleek."

"Where I'm from people don't change into animals, Crow."

"But you said he flew!"

"No, it's different where we're from. We have machines . . ." Mup sighed, too distracted by worry for her dad to try explaining about aeroplanes. "It's just different," she murmured.

The guards had gone very quiet and were also gazing tensely ahead. Ruined buildings were visible now among the trees: tumbled heaps of stone almost entirely overgrown by autumnal vines and bushes.

In the pendant, Aunty whispered very quietly.

Very quietly, the stones seemed to reply.

Are we almost there? wondered Mup.

Crow put his hand on her shoulder, startling her, and she turned to find him staring intently into her face. "I think you *can* change," he said. "Your little brother can, so why not you?"

Why not me? Mup thought of her surprising climb into the treetops; of the power which had only recently sparked at her fingertips.

"Try reaching inside you for the cat-shape," said Crow. "Like . . . like you were trying to remember a word. Reach inside and search for the cat-shape. Let it come out by itself . . ."

He drew back to give Mup room.

The guards eyed her warily. "Ho, boy," said the man. "He has them all at it now."

Mup shut her eyes, trying to blot out their disapproval. She concentrated on being a cat. To her amazement, it was right there—right beneath the surface—another Mup waiting to be brought out. Mup took a deep breath. She stretched out her hands and they were narrow and strong and tipped with claws ready for scratching. She unfolded her ears, long and sensitive, ready to hear the grass growing. She stretched one powerful back leg, then another, ready to run, ready to leap, ready to fight.

Her nose twitched, her eyes opened, and she looked up into Crow's horrified face.

"*By my tall hat!*" he exclaimed.

"*What possible use are you like that?*"

At Mup's neck, Aunty laughed.

Mup looked down to see the pendant glowing against the dark-brown fur of her chest. "Oh!" she said. "I'm not a cat at all! I'm a . . ."

"*The hare, the hare.*" Aunty's ghost laughed—thoroughly amused, it seemed. "*The stitcher of worlds!*"

"Where are my clothes?" asked Mup, standing on her hind legs and patting down her sleek brown body. She held her neat hands before her face. *Paws*, she thought, not displeased.

"A hare," muttered the male guard. "Of all the animals to choose. The queen very much disapproves of hares, she does. Wild, ungovernable things, always sniffing out alternatives, always going their own way and crossing boundaries." He shuddered. "You'll bring trouble down on yourself if you don't watch out."

All through this, his companion had been staring upstream as she steered the boat, her eyes wide with anxiety. Now she startled and said, "Look."

The man glanced up. His face fell, and he backed to her side. "We're here," he whispered.

Up ahead, a tall stone tower was visible above the golden treetops. Mup crept forward. The hands she gripped the cage with were human again: a small girl's dark hands. The face she pressed to the bars was a girl's face.

It's just around the corner, she thought. *Just around the next bend in the river.*

Grandma's house.

The guards were muttering frantically. "We need to explain very carefully. We can't make any mistakes. We need to get the words just right . . ."

"But I can't even look at one of the queen's creatures without thinking I've broken some law! They'll think we're guilty of something. We'll end up in the dungeons!"

"No, we won't. We . . . we just need to explain *carefully* and then . . ." The man made a frustrated noise. "Why am I so *scared?*" he cried. "I've done nothing *wrong!*"

"That never matters to her lot!"

"What will we do?"

There was a storm of desperate whispering in reply, and then the rustling of paper. Mup turned to find the frowning guards huddled together, the woman scribbling on a page torn from a notebook. Mup went back to watching the castle. More of it was becoming visible as the bend in the river approached. It was huge. Stretching far into the crowding forest and up into the clear blue sky.

Crow, a bird again, hopped to her shoulder, quietly chattering his beak and staring upwards. Tipper and Badger pressed close.

"Crow," said Mup quietly. "We must find a way to let Badger and Tipper out before—"

The raft tilted suddenly, sending them lurching into the bars of their cage. Then the boat began to turn with the current as if rudderless. Mup spun in time to see the guards leap for the shore. They transformed as they did so. In the blink of an eye, the man was airborne, carried up above the trees with one beat of his glossy wings. His companion landed fluidly on the riverbank, a slinky piebald cat. She stood for a moment looking at Mup with inscrutable emerald eyes, before turning away and blending with the forest shadows.

Tipper pressed his nose between the bars, staring after them. "They is gone," he said.

Badger whined.

Mup ran to check the padlock, which swung from the cage door. The guards had taken the keys. The gate was still locked fast. "Oh, Tipper," she whispered. "I think I've got you and Badger into terrible trouble."

The Queen's Keep

The water carried the raft around the bend in the river and into view of the castle. Everything was silent. The forest, which pressed right up against the square stone walls, was motionless. Even the water lapping at the castle's foundations did so quietly — as if afraid to draw attention to itself.

Mup's grip tightened on the bars of the cage. Her heart hammering, she gazed up and up as they moved into the castle's shadow.

Narrow steps led steeply from the river to a tall wooden gate that was the only opening in the looming cliff of wall. Raggedy witches lined these steps. Calm and motionless, dressed all in black, they waited with folded hands as the water carried the raft towards them.

At the head of the steps stood the familiar figure of Magda, straight-backed and imposing, the bright slash of silver shimmering in her dark hair. She seemed to be in charge. At her nod, the witches at the bottom of the steps reached out their pale arms. The cage was drawn in—as easily as if it were paper—and the lock was undone. Magda turned her back, disappearing under the gate arch, as the prisoners were herded from the boat.

Crow stayed as a bird, warily perched on Mup's shoulder. Tipper pressed warm to one side of her legs, Badger on the other, vigilant but very scared. Mup felt like the only human in the silent crowd of the queen's witches.

No one seemed curious or concerned by their presence. The witches were used to unloading cages of prisoners, it would seem, and they simply led the way through the gate.

The interior opened out before Mup: a large yard, hemmed on all sides by impossibly tall walls. High above, the sky was a distant square of blue, everything else was stone. Stairs were built into the walls, all leading upwards to firmly closed doors. Distant windows stared down.

We must look tiny from up there, thought Mup.

They moved quietly across the yard, their footsteps hardly dimpling the depth of the silence. Crow huddled closer to Mup's neck. The dogs pressed closer to her legs. The witches headed for an arched tunnel in the base of the far wall. It was a mouth of impenetrable darkness, and Mup realized she was allowing herself and her friends to be led towards it, docile as sheep.

"Hey," she said, stopping in her tracks. "Hey. Where are we going?"

Her voice was shockingly loud. It rang back from the walls like a bell.

The witches simply stared at her, stone-faced, and pushed to get her moving again.

"No!" she cried, shrugging them off. "I'm here to see the queen."

Again a hand pressed to Mup's back, shoving her forwards. Badger growled, snapping. Crow pecked, and the witches withdrew. Too angry now to even be afraid, Mup broke free of their ranks, shoving back out into the open space of the yard. She spun to look up at the high and watchful windows.

"HEY!" she yelled. "HEY UP THERE! TELL THE QUEEN HER GRANDDAUGHTER IS HERE! TELL HER I WANT TO TALK TO HER!"

One of the witches pushed through the others to Magda, who had been standing at a distance, emotionlessly observing. "Ma'am," he said, offering the scrap of paper which the guards had left pinned to the cage. "There is a note."

Magda took it, frowning. "The heir's child," she said, reading the note. "How useful. Now we have both child and husband to draw her in."

"So you do have my dad!" cried Mup.

"Yes," murmured Magda without looking up. "And if the heir ever wants to see either of you again, she will have to come here. Let us see how well she fares when she has to do battle on our home ground." She crumpled the note with distaste. "I should never have allowed your mother to stay in the mundane world. The queen said she was only feigning disinterest in the throne, and she was right. I should have known she'd sneak back across the border as soon as she could, looking to stir up trouble."

"Mam is not looking for trouble," cried Mup. "She just wants Dad back. Then we'll go home."

Suddenly, Crow—who had been ignoring this conversation, his eyes fixed on the distant windows—cawed from his perch on Mup's shoulder. "DAD! DAD! I'M HERE! CAN YOU HEAR ME?"

At his voice, Magda looked up. At first she seemed startled by Crow, maybe even afraid, but when Crow—not noticing her—kept yelling, her face drew down with anger, and she stalked forward.

Mup backed away, carrying Crow with her and all the time shouting up at the distant windows. "HEY! HEY UP THERE! TELL THE QUEEN I WANT HER!"

Magda grabbed. Mup ducked, still yelling. But it was Crow the witch wanted, and she snatched him from Mup's shoulder, cruelly clamping his beak shut with one hand. She wrapped her other hand firmly around his neck. "Shut up!" she hissed. "Shut up, you appalling little brat!"

Mup, horrified that the woman was about to wring Crow's neck, leapt for her. The dogs barked and jumped. The witches closed in, and within moments, Mup found herself held fast by a multitude of pale hands. Tipper yelped and Badger struggled, but they were muzzled in a moment and shackled together with heavy collars and chains. Feathers flew as Crow fought, but it was not long before his beak was bound shut and his leg tied to a heavy weight.

"Be quiet!" growled Magda in his ear. "I'm warning you!"

Crow looked up into her pale, angry face for the first time. His eyes widened, and he grew still.

Magda snarled to her companions, "Take these miscreants to the dungeons. Now!"

"I WANT THE QUEEN!" yelled Mup as she and the dogs were dragged towards the dark tunnel. "I WANT MY GRANDMOTHER!"

Someone cuffed her ear. Someone loomed, a gag poised to tie around her mouth.

A voice rang down from the walls above — "CEASE THIS SPECTACLE!" — and everyone froze.

Mup strained to see. Was this her grandmother? Was this the queen, at last?

A woman, distant on the balconied landing of a vertiginous staircase, looked down on them. The witches seemed to contract at the sight of her, pulling in towards each other as if for strength.

They're afraid of her, thought Mup.

The woman's voice came trickling down like ice water on the ringing air. "What is this noise?" she asked.

Magda stepped forward, Crow motionless and staring in her hands. "P-prisoners, Majesty. Claiming kinship and right to audience."

The distant figure of the woman leaned over the

balcony, better to see. Long white hair fell forward. It was impossible to tell her expression from so far away. She straightened. "Bring them up," she said, and she disappeared into one of the many doors above.

Up and up and up the narrow steps they climbed, with witches ahead of them and witches behind. Mup marched resolutely, Tipper and Badger panting at her heels, Magda leading the way. Crow was still clutched tightly in her hand. He came and went from Mup's view with the swinging of the witch's arm He had the weight which was designed to hold him down gripped in his foot like a weapon. A band of leather held his beak cruelly shut, but over the top of it, his bright eyes roamed the walls and closed doors and many dark windows, searching all the time for signs of his father.

The picture was still fresh in Mup's mind of her own father, limp in the arms of these witches, borne away on a pillar of smoke. *Are you really here, Dad?* she thought. *Please be here.*

She wondered where Mam was. She must have been frantic when she realized Sealgaire had taken her children so far from her. She must have been raging. Mup could imagine her now, stalking across this world, lightning at her fingertips, dark eyes aflame, searching for her daughter, searching for her son and her husband. It made Mup feel stronger to know that, out there, someone like Mam cared about her and wanted her and was looking for her.

She reached with her mind, but she couldn't find a connection anywhere in this still, silent place that might lead to her parents. It would have been terrific to have a phone line down which she could send her thoughts, or maybe — as seemed to work in this place — a tree or some bare earth on which to place her hands. Without something like that, Mup's mind had nowhere solid to direct itself, and she was detached from the web of connections she usually felt a part of.

Still climbing upwards, Mup discreetly spread her hands. Sparks pinpricked her fingers.

What would she do to make the queen give Dad back — hit her? Mup had never hit anyone in her life; it had never been something she'd had to consider doing. Now she had summoned fire to her palms, ready to throw it, ready to burn with it if necessary.

Is this right? she thought. *I don't think this is right. People shouldn't have to throw fire at each other.* She looked at Crow, bound and helpless before her. She heard Tipper and Badger behind her, panting under the weight of their chains. Her grandmother had done that to them. Her grandmother had had her dad locked up in jail.

Mup moved her fingers gently as she thought this, allowing the sparks to dance.

All the way up the stairs, Aunty whispered and muttered in the pendant around Mup's neck, but there was no reply. The stones here were silent. At the top of the stairs, as Magda led Mup in under the door arch and out of the sunshine, Aunty fell silent too.

The queen sat herself down into a hard chair as Mup was herded into the room. There was a lot of brightly polished white marble floor between them, and as Mup crossed it, the queen had ample time to look her up and down. Distaste and disapproval grew in her elderly face. Mup was reminded of a time at school when a group of girls had surrounded her and called her names. Back then, she had felt a shrivelling feeling in her stomach when she realized that those girls didn't like her, that there would never be anything she could do to make them like her. Now, walking across the floor to meet her grandmother for the very first time, Mup felt the same shrinking feeling—the feeling that she was useless and stupid, the feeling that no one had ever really loved her.

The sparks retreated into her fingertips.

"Ma'am," said Magda. "This is your granddaughter."

"Granddaughter?" said the queen. "*Grand*daughter?" She made a show of peering at Mup. Her face was Aunty Boo's face, but without any of Aunty Boo's dry humour or kindness: a cold face, a sneering face. She tutted. "There seems to be nothing *grand* about this daughter that I can see. What even *is* she?"

"She's a girl!" woofed Tipper, as if the queen honestly needed to be told.

"She's a sad little, silly little, useless scrap of nothing, if appearances are anything to go by," huffed the queen. "It's beyond comprehension that she's even remotely related to me." She addressed herself to Mup for the first time, leaning forward in her chair so that her long white hair fell around her face. "Look at you—you mixed-up jumble of human wastage—with your little circus troupe of friends and your rabbit hat and your silly dress. Where exactly do you think you are, a *tea party*?"

That's not fair, thought Mup. *I'm not wastage, and I like my friends, and what does my dress have to do with anything?*

But her cheeks flared, and she felt useless and ridiculous, and she wished—despite herself—that she'd worn something more sensible than a tutu and green frog wellies to come and rescue her dad. She found herself thinking, *Maybe then the queen might have liked me.*

The queen sat back, bitterly satisfied with herself. "It's obvious my sister has *ruined* your mother, if you're anything to go by, you frilly little doll."

And that made Mup angry again. Because she knew for a fact that Mam was *wonderful* and that Aunty had *not* ruined her—and who cared what this stranger thought about anything? Mup had *power in her hands*. Mup was *here for a reason*. (And she could dress whatever way she wanted to rescue her dad, damn it! And she loved her friends and that was that.)

"Give me my dad," she said.

The queen laughed. "Or what? What will you do if I say no?"

"She'll zap you!" barked Tipper enthusiastically. "Like she done the birdy-man! And I'll snap you with my teeth like I done the nasty cat-lady who scratched me!"

The queen lost all her amusement. "Zap?" she said. "Snap?"

Magda loomed over Mup. "That was you?" she hissed. "You were the one who burned my brother?"

The queen's attention snapped to Magda. "Brother?" she said.

Magda faltered and stepped back from Mup. Her face went as pale as the streak in her hair. "N-no," she stammered. "I-I mean . . ."

"But, Magda," said the queen, her voice suddenly smooth as silk, "you said 'brother.' Am I not your only family, Magda? Are you not loyal to me? Are you not faithful only to me?"

"No, Majesty. I mean, yes! YES, Majesty. I am loyal to you only. Only you, Majesty."

"Because you took an oath, you know."

"Oh, I know, Majesty." The witch held up her hands, almost begging. "And I meant every word, Majesty. There is only you. You are everything. All else is cast away."

"So who is this 'brother' the tinselly scrap is supposed to have burned?"

"I didn't burn anyone," said Mup. But even as she said it, her hands tingled with the memory of pressing themselves to Sealgaire's chest; of shooting fire so that he and she were flung away from each other.

"He deserved it!" barked Tipper. "He was being mean to you."

"Oh, no," whispered Mup, staring at her hands. "He was only trying to help . . ." She remembered quickly covering the imprint of her own hands on Sealgaire's chest. She had seen yet not allowed herself to see the evidence of the damage she had done to him. "I didn't mean it," she whispered — but she had. She *had* meant it. At the time she had only wanted to escape the grip of whoever was holding her. In the heat of battle she had recognized only an enemy — and so she had hurt someone who was trying to help her.

Tipper was very excited now and barking at the top of his voice. "He was a mean, mean birdy-man! He was mean to Aunty and he was mean to Crow too!"

"Crow?" said the queen. "*Crow?*" She turned her attention to Crow, who had stayed very quiet through all this, clutched in Magda's hand, staring up into her now panic-stricken face.

At the sight of him, the queen smiled a thin amused smile. "Say it isn't so," she said.

Magda tried to hide Crow behind her back.

The queen lifted very cold eyes to meet hers.

"Magda," she said. "Put that raven onto the ground and make him take his boy-form."

The witch shook her head like a frightened child being accused of something they hadn't done. "I didn't bring him here, Majesty. If I had known . . ."

"Put. The raven. Onto. The floor."

Reluctantly Magda obeyed. The stone tied to Crow's foot clinked as she placed him on the ground. The queen regarded him with malevolent glee, but Crow couldn't seem to take his eyes from Magda's face. Above the leather band constricting his beak, his round, dark eyes were full of tears.

"Let's see you," said the queen.

When Crow continued to just stare, the queen pointed her finger. "Let's *see* you."

With a *zap*, Crow's bonds were gone and he was revealed: a small scruffy boy standing on the polished marble floor. "Mother," he cried to Magda. "Mam!"

Oh, no! thought Mup in horror. Was this awful person really his mother?

Crow held his hands out to Magda.

The witch winced, and the queen grinned. "Oh, Magda," she said. "Be sure your weaknesses will seek you out! Have you kept this child hidden like a kitten in a cupboard? All these years, have you cherished

the thought of him way down deep in your senti-
mental soul?"

"Where's Dad?" cried Crow. "Mam, where is he?
Sealgaire said you arrested him!"

The queen was delighted. "Where's my *daddy?*"
she whined in mocking imitation. "Where's he *gone?*
What a baby!" She laughed, and all her witches
laughed with her, the horrible crystalline sound
bouncing off the stone surfaces of the room like ice
shattering.

Under the sting of this laughter, Magda's face
grew expressionless and she drew herself up.

The queen spoke slyly to her. "You can always go
back, Magda. If you want. You can have your kitten.
You can once again be part of the squirming rabble."
She spread her hands generously. "Just give up the
use of magic and I'll let you walk away."

Magda met the queen's eyes. "I would rather die,"
she said.

The queen smiled her awful smile. She turned to
Crow. "Your *daddy* is dead," she said.

Crow grabbed Magda's cloak, begging her to con-
tradict the queen. But Magda would not look at him.

"Your father brought it on himself," Magda said.
"He was a traitor and a rebel."

"And your mammy knows what to do with rebels," said the queen. "Don't you, Magda?"

"Yes," said Magda, and again she said, "He brought it on himself."

Crow began to cry.

"You killed Crow's dad," gasped Mup. "You horrible person!"

She leapt forward, not knowing what she intended to do, wanting only to punish this awful cold woman who stood over her weeping son like he meant nothing at all. She was caught and restrained by the witches. They yanked her arms over her head, so that the sparks that gushed from her palms blasted harmlessly upwards, where they left scorch marks on the ceiling.

The queen regarded Mup more closely than before. "Interesting," she said. "For all her frivolous exterior, there's something there. A little seed of potential perhaps, not yet smothered by my sister." She leaned forward. She flicked a hand. "Let me see what you are," she said.

Mup felt something jolt inside her—something rising like a bubble within—and suddenly she was on all fours looking down at her long, narrow paws, the angry face of a hare reflected back at her in the shining marble.

The witches gasped and drew back. The queen recoiled in horror.

"A hare?" she roared. "A *stitcher of worlds?* In my own family? From my own *blood?*"

She rose to her feet, her white hair crackling in rage, her eyes ablaze.

"There is only *one path,*" she hissed. "Do you understand? Every other path leads *nowhere.* I will not have my own blood, issue of my issue, daughter of my *daughter,* imply otherwise! There is only *one way*—in magic, in life, in love—and that way is *me.* All magic comes from me, all love centres on me, all obedience is due to *me.*"

She seemed to grow with rage, and Mup scampered away, her sharp nails skittering on the floor. In her panic, she found herself entangled in the legs and chains of the snarling dogs. She tried to change back into a girl but was stuck in her animal form, from fear, perhaps, or some terrible will of the queen.

"Get her out of my sight!" roared the queen. "Corrupt, polluted, irregular girl! Lock her away!"

Mup was lifted, bucking and kicking and biting with her sharp teeth. The world went dark as someone wrapped her in their thick cloak. Still struggling, she was carried outside. Sunlight came prickling through the fabric and footsteps rang from stone as she was carried down and down and down many sunlit steps with the dogs barking close behind.

There was no sound from Crow.

Mup's angry cries echoed from high walls as she was carried across the open yard. Then there was darkness: the feeling of damp space that had never known light. Sounds closed in. Coldness. The dogs grew quiet. Mup stilled, listening to the jogging breath of the people around her and the clink of the dogs' chains. Tipper whimpered.

They went down and down, the air growing colder even through the fabric that bundled her. They came to a halt. There came the rattle of keys. Metal shrieked against metal in the dark as something like a great gate opened reluctantly. Mup was shaken violently free of the cloak and she rolled across a damp stone floor, the breath knocked from her.

The sound of the gate came again, screeching closed even as she scrambled to her feet. Mup ran for it, a girl once more, but by the time she'd crossed the darkness, the witches were gone.

There was a familiar chattering of beak behind her.

Mup turned, her back pressed to the metal bars

of the cell door. She could see nothing. The darkness was complete.

"Crow?" she whispered. "T-Tipper?"

Suddenly the air was filled with the rush of wings, and Mup ducked and raised her hands as some panicked thing brushed her face. "Crow!" she cried as he began battering himself against the unyielding bars of the gate. "Stop!" But he was already off again, tumbling frantically into the dark. Mup heard him hit the ceiling, fall, then flutter back into the air. He was silent except for the desperate beating of his wings, and the thud thud thud of his body against the cell walls.

There came an especially loud thud, and the sounds ceased abruptly.

Tipper's voice came from the darkness, small and terrified. "Has the birdy hurted himself?"

Mup groped her way forward. It wasn't long until she met the back wall of the cell, the stones cold and damp against her outstretched hands.

"Crow?" she whispered.

Her foot bumped something soft. She knelt and felt the worn cloth of a threadbare coat, a skinny arm, a trembling back. "Crow," she whispered again. He was lying at the base of the wall. "Are you hurt?"

He did not answer, but she could tell from the shaking of his body that he was crying. "You're not alone, Crow," she said, though she too had started crying now. "You're not alone."

She tried to pull him into her arms, but he elbowed her away.

"Crow," she said, almost pleading. She chanced putting her hand on his arm. He curled tighter, but he didn't draw any further from her than that, and so she sank to the stones, her back against the wall, her hand on his quivering shoulder.

The witches must have removed the dogs' chains because Mup did not hear them creep forward, and they gave her a fright when their warm breath first hit her face. Badger licked her cheek—a little doggy kiss—then he and Tipper lay their warm bodies on either side of her and Crow, protecting them from the cold.

Mup pulled Tipper in so that she was hugging him with one arm. Badger lay his head on her lap. "Don't worry, everyone," she said, the tears running down her face invisible in the dark. "Don't worry. I'll think of something."

A Glowing
Path

After a very long time, Crow cried himself to sleep. Then Tipper fell asleep, and soon Badger was snoring softly. Mup was left wide awake. "Aunty Boo," she whispered. "Are you still here?"

The pendant flickered, its glow barely penetrating the dark.

"Aunty, I was the one who hurt Sealgaire. It was my fault he couldn't sit up properly, and fell so far, and . . . and died."

The pendant sighed. *"Poor Sealgaire . . ."*

"I'm sorry I hurt him, Aunty. I'm *so* sorry. I want not to have done it. I was scared. I didn't know who he was. I . . ."

"That's the thing about power. It has consequences outside of yourself — you have to be very sure before you use it that you're

doing something you won't regret. Because once you've used it, there's no going back."

Mup hugged Tipper tighter, thinking how little her regret meant to Sealgaire; how her being sorry changed nothing for him. She shivered. Tipper whimpered in his sleep.

"Aunty," said Mup. "I don't know where Mam is. What if . . . what if she can't find us? What about poor Tipper? What about Badger and Crow? What'll become of them, down here in the dark?"

"Most people who end up here never see the light of day again."

Mup groaned in horror. "Don't say that, Aunty."

The pendant sighed. "I abandoned them. All those brave souls too stubborn or too different to conform to my sister's rules. So many of them died here. So many ghosts in these stones."

Mup clutched the pendant at her neck, suddenly terrified that the darkness might begin to swarm with the luminous dead.

The pendant pulsed slightly, and it felt as if Aunty was smiling now, gently smiling, at the small girl imprisoned in the dark, in the cold and the damp beneath miles of stone. "I can't pretend I'm not delighted at how much you upset my sister. My darling Pearl, a hare! A stitcher of worlds."

"What are you talking about?" cried Mup. "The stitcher of worlds? I can't even sew!"

"Oh, child," tutted Aunty. "Not sewing. Stitching! Stitching. You are a hare. A border creature. Neither quite one thing or another, the best of all worlds, and always only ever yourself. Hares see both sides, they find their own path. No wonder my sister hates and fears you."

"Does she really hate me?"

"She hates everyone, Pearl. No one's ever good enough for her. You'd grind yourself to dust trying to please her. There's always only ever been one way to do things with her. 'My way or the hangman,' if you know what I mean."

"A bit like you with Mam?"

There was a long silence from the pendant. "I don't know what you mean."

"Yes, you do," said Mup.

"I love your mam! I've always done what's best for her!"

"I-I know," said Mup, starting to wish she'd not said anything.

"Sometimes she doesn't know what's good for her, is all. I had to keep a lid on her a little bit . . . Stop things flying out of control."

"Wouldn't it have been better, though," ventured Mup, "to just trust Mam and teach her how to be herself?"

"She'd never have been able for that!" cried Aunty. "Why are you all so ungrateful all of a sudden? I made you all a lovely life! I know what's good for you!"

Mup said nothing. The pendant went very quiet. To Mup's alarm, Aunty's light began to fade. "Aunty . . . ? Aunty, I didn't mean it. You're always very nice to Mam. She loves you! I love you too." Mup shook the darkening pendant. "Don't be angry!"

"I need a moment to myself," said Aunty faintly. "I—I need to think . . ."

The light fluttered, then died entirely. Aunty's voice died with it, and no matter how hard Mup shook the pendant, neither the light nor Aunty came back.

Darkness pressed in, cold and impenetrable.

For a moment Mup was too scared to move, then she was angry. Really angry.

How could Aunty have just left her like that? Come to think of it, how could her mam have left her? And her dad? They were adults, for goodness' sake! Weren't they meant to keep their daughter safe? Weren't they meant to take care of her—not leave her stuck in a dungeon underground with poor neglected Crow, and poor innocent Tipper, and poor Badger, who was too old for things like this?

Mup was suddenly too angry to stay still. If she

had to lie there another minute, she'd scream in rage, and Mup knew this would terrify her friends. She would rather be on her own in the dark than risk upsetting Crow and Tipper any further, so she slipped out from under their warmth and crawled away.

Face scrunched up, angry tears streaming down her cheeks, Mup could have kept moving forever, but soon she reached the iron bars of the gate and had to stop. "I don't like you," she whispered to the grandmother who had put her there. "I don't *care* if you hate me. You're wicked and you hurt people and you don't deserve to be my granny."

She closed her hands around the bars of the gate. "What's wrong with being a hare anyway?" she said. "I like being a hare." And, as if to prove it, her body became one.

The world flared to sight in shifting whorls of grey and white.

What a difference! Mup thought, looking around in wonder. *I can see!*

Standing on her hind legs, she examined the iron gate. Its bars were close enough together that even the slimmest animal couldn't slip through. A heavy lock fastened it tight. Outside, the walls of the narrow corridor seeped damp. To Mup's new vision all was dim and colourless, like trying to peer at a black-and-white movie through a thick fog.

Mup turned and looked back into the cell. It had felt very large when all she could see was darkness, but it wasn't large at all. Crow and Tipper and Badger were huddled together at the back wall. In his sleep, Crow had thrown his arms around Tipper's neck. Tipper had his head on Crow's shoulder. Badger curled around them both, a stiff, old, grey-muzzled knight. Mup felt very protective of them, and her anger faded. This must be how her mam felt when she looked at her and Tipper.

Mup sat down slowly. Her mam hadn't left her, not really. They'd been taken from each other, they'd been *separated*. Before that they'd been working together. Acting as a team to find Mup's dad, who had also been taken. *No one abandoned me*, thought Mup, gazing at Crow. *No one purposely left me on my own.*

She remembered Mam standing at the steps of Sealgaire's wagon, smiling gravely up at her. *"Keep yourself out of trouble,"* she'd said. *"Take care of your little brother."* And she'd trusted Mup to do just that, she'd believed in her to do just that. Mup closed her eyes, knowing once again that Mam was out there, trusting that she would come for her. *I'm here, Mam,* she thought. *I'm being brave. I'm taking care of everyone. I'll do my best until you get to us.*

A soft noise in the corridor caused her to shrink carefully back against the wall. Someone was approaching from the foggy dimness, someone tall. They held in their outstretched hand a luminous orb, which cast a dim glow of light on the walls and ceiling. Every couple of feet this orb dripped, for all the world like a candle dripping melting wax. When a drip hit the floor, it glowed like a tiny flame. Peering past the advancing figure, Mup could see a series of these luminous points stretching back into the corridor, leaving a path through the impenetrable darkness.

The tall figure came to a halt at the door of the cell. It was Crow's mother. Now that she was closer, Mup could see that she wasn't holding the orb of light but making it—gently rubbing the fingertips of one hand together to generate an almost solid bubble of illumination. The light brightened her expressionless features as she hunted in the folds of her flowing robe. She did not notice Mup cowering on the other side of the bars. Mup crept slowly backwards as Magda produced a huge key from her pocket, clicked the lock, and swung open the cell door.

"Boy," she said.

At the back of the cell, Crow startled, and Mup saw him clutch Tipper and Badger. All of them were awake now, staring wide-eyed at the coldly illuminated woman standing in the corridor.

"I have made a path for you," said the witch, "that you might find your way out."

Crow leapt to his feet, his pinched face bright with joy. "Mam!" he cried. "You came for me!" He ran across the room, his arms out to hug her. But before he could touch her, his mother held up her free hand and brought him to a halt.

"I want you to leave me alone," she said. "I want you to go and never come back."

She waited a moment, perhaps to witness the crumbling of hope from her son's face. Then she turned her back and walked away. Her orb cast a cold bubble of illumination as she ascended into the darkness, then was gone. Crow was left in the feeble light of the pathway she had made for him, staring after her.

"Mam," he whispered.

Quietly, Mup stood up into her girl-shape. Without her see-in-the-dark hare-vision, the corridor shrank to just the thin trail of light cast by the luminous path. The darkness outside it was absolute, but Mup now knew that the darkness contained rooms and doors, long corridors of empty stone. She knew that, with an effortless twist of her will, she could easily find her way through it. Tipper and Badger came to her sides, their soft muzzles touching her hands.

Crow stood with his back to them all, his shoulders rigid, his gaze fixed on the emptiness ahead.

"We'll be your family, Crow," said Mup.

Crow spun to her. His eyes were dry of tears.

Mup faltered at his fierce expression. "I mean . . ." she stammered. "I mean, we'll be your family if you want us to be. I know we're a little bit strange. Mam can be kind of scary, and Dad isn't around much. Also, Aunty is a ghost and Tipper is a dog, but maybe if you gave us a try you might . . ."

She didn't get a chance to say any more because Crow flung himself at her, and her words were choked by how hard he hugged her.

"I . . . I'd like to try and find my dad now," said Mup at last. "Is that OK?"

Crow nodded against her shoulder.

"It means going into the dark, though. Is that OK?"

Crow stepped away from her, fiercely wiping his eyes and nodding.

"Tipper? Badger? Do you trust me to lead you through the dark?"

The dogs licked her fingers. *Yes.*

"OK," said Mup.

She dropped into her hare-shape and turned her back on the path Crow's mother had left for them. The corridor stretched ahead for eight or nine feet before fading to grey. The cells on either side were empty. Mup hopped forward, sniffing the air for signs of danger, or maybe traces of her dad's aftershave.

Tipper's voice came from behind her. "Mup? How is we meant to follow, if we can't see you?"

She turned to find the others standing where she'd left them, peering blindly after her without moving. "Can't you see in the dark when you are animals?" she asked.

As one they shook their heads. The light of Magda's path glowed dimly behind them, making a silhouette of their anxious little huddle. Mup hopped to the nearest little splotch of light. The others watched as she tentatively touched it. Her paw came up glowing, as if covered with luminous paint.

"Come here, guys," she said. "I have an idea."

Corridor after corridor of cold, dark cells stretched ahead of them and behind them. All empty, all silent except for the soft padding of their paws and the *tap-tap* of Crow's shoes as they moved from room to room.

Where are all the prisoners? thought Mup. *Where is my dad?* She shuddered and looked back the way she'd come.

Tipper, Badger, and Crow were following close behind. Streaked with Magda's paint, they were glowing like so many strange little ghosts. Mup had painted her long ears and her face so that her friends could see her in the dark. Every place they touched, they left neat paw prints or handprints that glowed behind them, a faint smudged trail leading back the way they'd come. It would not be difficult to find their way out.

Crow kept looking back at this trail, fretting. He had told Mup that he was worried the witches would see it and follow it and find them. But Mup knew the witches rarely came this deep anymore. She found it hard to explain how she knew this. It was as if the stones themselves were sharing their knowledge. All Mup had to do was press her paws to the ground and concentrate, and all the journeys that had ever been taken here, all the paths ever trod, spread themselves out before her as clear as a network of maps.

The stitcher of worlds, she thought. *The finder of paths.*

She became more certain with every step that this still, sad, empty darkness was rarely disturbed. Whoever the witches brought down here — to the very depths of the castle — was left here and forgotten about and never mentioned nor thought of again.

This is what the queen would have done to us, she thought. *Me and Crow and Badger and Tipper. No one would ever have found us. No one would ever have come for us. We'd have been left all alone in this darkness, and we'd never have been seen again.*

"I smell Daddy," whispered Tipper suddenly, his eyes brightening in the strange light.

Mup paused, sniffing the air.

Crow sniffed too. "Does he smell like damp?" he asked.

"No," cried Mup in excitement, already turning and leading the way. "He smells like Christmas trees!"

"And warm milk!" woofed Tipper, pushing past Crow to follow on her heels.

"And toast!"

"And butter!"

"And apple tart!"

They ran down the corridor, shouting out all the happy things their dad smelled of, with Badger and Crow following warily behind, until they came to a halt at an unfurnished cell. Inside, a lone occupant sat on the floor, staring in bewilderment at the glowing creatures who suddenly filled his doorway.

"Well," said Dad in his familiar voice. "Hello."

"Dad?" asked Mup. "What are you doing just sitting there?"

Her dad looked down at himself, and then all around him at the empty cell. "I think," he said, in mild surprise, "I think I'm just waiting." He didn't seem at all unhappy, though his face was bruised and his hair all tangled, and the flight suit he still wore was torn and filthy and damp. Mup got the impression that he had simply been sitting there in the dark, perfectly content, until they'd turned up to surprise him with their light. The door to his cell wasn't even closed.

"Dad," she said. "Don't you want to escape?"

He thought deeply. "Do I?" he asked.

"Yes!" barked Tipper. "You do!"

"Oh," said Dad. "Well . . . OK. If you say so."

"He's under a glamour," whispered Crow.

"A what?"

"A spell. I'd wager he doesn't even know where he is."

Mup hopped into the room and looked up into her dad's pleasant, puzzled face. "It's OK, Dad," she said. "We're here to rescue you."

Dad nodded, smiling, and peered past her. "Who's this?" he asked.

"That's Badger, our dog."

"And this?"

"That's Tipper. He's your son."

"Oh. And he's a dog too, is he?"

"Yes. Sometimes."

"And who's that, lurking at the door?"

"That's Crow. He's a boy, sometimes. He's going to be our brother one day . . ."

Crow greeted this observation with a scowl.

"Though, perhaps he hasn't quite made up his mind about that yet," added Mup quickly.

"Pleased to meet you, Crow," said Dad, rising to his feet and offering his hand. Crow flinched back as if suspecting some trick, but Dad just kept his hand out, smiling expectantly, and eventually Crow came forward. As he and Dad shook hands, Mup was pleased to see some of the suspicion melt from Crow's face.

To her surprise, Dad turned his questioning smile back to her. "And who are you, little rabbit?"

"I'm Mup," she cried indignantly. "Your *daughter*."

"She not a wabbit," barked Tipper. "She's a hare."

Dad nodded and smiled. "I see. I see," he said, but it was obvious he was just being polite.

"He'll be more sensible when you get him home," Crow assured her. "Though I'm not sure how we're going to manage it," he said. "It's not like there's a back door we can sneak him out of."

"We're just going to have to go back up into the castle," said Mup. "Trust that your mam's path will lead us somewhere safe."

They all looked upwards, as if they could see through the many fathoms of stone ceiling to the queen and all her witches, who prowled the world above.

"And then what?" whispered Tipper.

"We . . . we'll think of that when we get there," said Mup firmly, shepherding them out into the corridor. "Let's go."

To her surprise, Dad shrank back from the

threshold of the door. "I'd better not. That woman . . . the old woman who put me here . . . I don't think she wants me to leave." He shuddered, obviously afraid. "I—I don't want to make her angry again . . ."

Mup hopped back into the cell. "Dad?"

But her dad shook his head and retreated to the wall and turned his face away.

Mup stood up into her girl-shape. The room shrank immediately to utter blackness. She couldn't see her dad at all, and she was filled with panic suddenly at how dark it was and how cold and confined, and how deeply underground they were.

A glow of light appeared at the corner of her eye as Badger, Crow, and Tipper returned to the door of the cell. Their luminous faces shed only a hint of light, and Mup was filled with astonishment and admiration as she realized just how little her friends had been able to see while she'd been hopping along in happy security with her special vision.

"Thanks for coming with me, guys," she said.

"Wouldn't mind getting out now," grumbled Crow.

Dad shuffled behind her, and Mup lifted her luminous hands, bringing him dimly into view.

"Dad," she said gently.

He glanced at her over his shoulder, then turned

towards her as he registered her newly transformed face. "Oh," he said. "You're . . . you're a little girl."

"Sometimes I am," she said.

She held her hand out to him, and after a moment's hesitation he took it. "Come on, Dad," she said, lifting her free arm up like a feeble torch to light his way. "Let's go."

They made their way up and up, following the smudged trail of their own footprints. This time it was the dogs and Crow who led the way through the maze of corridors, while Mup stumbled after them, holding her dad's hand tightly, her eyes strained against the pressing gloom. Somewhere in the darkest recesses, before they reached the brighter trail left by Crow's mother, Aunty began muttering and stirring within the confines of her pendant. The darkness around them began to shift and shimmer with ghostly replies.

"What's that noise?" whispered her dad.

Mup clutched his hand tighter. "I think it's Aunty," she said. "Talking to the dead."

"Aunty," mused her dad. "I knew an Aunty once. She was very kind to my wife."

"Walk faster, Dad."

"She hadn't much time for me, though. Not once the babies were here. She was done with me then, I think . . . though I still liked her."

"Keep walking."

"My wife loved her very much."

"Keep *walking*."

"Who . . . who are you again, little girl?"

Mup just tugged his hand, desperate to hurry his pace. The pendant was buzzing now. The stones in the walls gasped and grated. In the darkness, dust sifted down.

The ghosts are angry, thought Mup, hurrying to catch up with the dogs and Crow. "We did nothing to you!" she cried out. "It wasn't us!"

"My fault," whispered Aunty. *"Mine, mine, mine."*

"No!" cried Mup, clutching the pendant with her free hand to silence it, running now through the growing frenzy of noise. "Shhh!"

"Follow her. Follow," whispered Aunty. *"Follow the hare into the light."*

"Aunty! No!"

"I smell outside!" barked Tipper, and they skidded around the corner to find themselves looking up a long flight of stone steps to a distant patch of sunlight. Stunned by the sweet draught of fresh air coming from above, the dogs and Crow came to a halt. Mup raced up behind and shoved them urgently up the steps.

"Climb!" she yelled. "Can't you hear that noise? The corridor is coming down around us!"

They scrambled clumsily upwards, Mup dragging Dad in their wake. All around them the stones were jolting and grinding. The pendant was burning around her neck. Ghost voices were wailing now, from deep below, howling out their rage. Mup ran up and up, her face turned to the little patch of sunlight, and as she climbed she became aware of other sounds, not so ghostly, coming from the world above them: shouts and great concussive boomings; the rush of a storm; a singing like that of wind through telephone wires; and above it all, a woman's voice—huge, magnificent, powerful—commanding:

"GIVE THEM TO ME. GIVE THEM TO ME. GIVE ME WHAT IS MINE."

Memory Finds a Voice

They emerged into the castle yard. Wind snatched their hair. Light stunned their eyes. For a moment all five companions — Mup, Crow, the dogs, and Dad — were frozen in terror. The yard was filled with hundreds of raggedy witches, all their pale faces turned upwards, their arms pointed high as they calmly shot fire into the sky. There was a sense of vast movement overhead, storm clouds boiling, perhaps, or a huge figure prowling.

Mup realized that the storm which raged around them was singing: a beautiful, terrible harmony of voices which seemed to come from somewhere outside the walls.

Combined magics, she thought in awe.

The song was creating the storm, and the storm was unpicking the defences of the castle. Howling through the yard where silence had reigned for so long, it was lifting the very stones themselves from the walls and shooting them into the sky.

Mup's grandmother stood in the centre of the yard, her arms stretched to the clouds, her face taut with concentration. She was tracking something up there with her outstretched hands — the same way a hunter traces the movement of a bird with a gun.

Mam, thought Mup with a jolt. *She's hunting Mam!*

"No!" Mup yelled, releasing her father's hand and running out into the yard. "MAM!"

But her voice was a little thread against the great choir of the storm. Not even the raggedy witches looked her way.

"Muuuup!" howled Tipper. "What am you dooooing?"

She waved him back, gesturing for Crow and Dad to keep the dogs by the wall and out of range of the flying stones. Out in the yard, the queen tensed suddenly and crouched and flexed her hands. She'd spotted her prey in the clouds above.

"Shoot her!" yelled Crow to Mup, struggling to

keep Badger from running into the fray. "Shoot the queen!"

Instead, Mup slapped her hands to her temples. She closed her eyes. She became very quiet.

On some level she could still feel the storm whipping at her hair and her clothes. She could hear the choir lifting the stones. But that was far away. She was a calm stillness at the heart of the chaos. She was the bridge, she was the conduit, she was the stitcher of worlds. Mup reached her thoughts to the great creature prowling the clouds above her and closed the gap between its mind and hers.

Mam, she thought.

There was a pause in the movement overhead.

Move, urged Mup. *Now.*

And though the creature above her was so strong now, and so angry that it hardly knew what lay below it anymore, it did as Mup told it. The queen's lightning zapped the air where the creature had been only moments before, missing it by a fraction and turning the clouds there to steam. There was a sense of the great creature turning to its companions, of it sweeping up its arm. *Draw back a moment*, it seemed to say, *there's something down there I don't quite —*

The connection broke, and Mup gasped and

staggered, spots dancing before her eyes. *Goodness, she thought, that was a lot harder than finding someone through a phone line.*

"MUP!" cried Crow. "LOOK OUT!"

The queen had turned Mup's way. The ranks of her witches did the same, their pale faces expressionless, their dark eyes staring. Overhead the clouds churned and funnelled as the creature there dropped out of sight beyond the castle walls, to where the unseen choir was still singing. Without taking her eyes from Mup, the queen signalled to the raggedy witches. They turned away and resumed firing at the storm, which had once again begun dismantling the walls of the castle.

The queen stalked towards Mup. She seemed to grow as she did so, and soon she was looming over her, impossibly tall, her white hair crackling around her angry face. "I should have killed your mother in the cradle," she boomed. "I should have known she'd grow up and try and take my throne." Her voice was immense and terrible, and very like the voice of the creature which now prowled the clouds above.

"Mam doesn't want your throne," cried Mup. "She just wants me and Tipper and Dad."

The queen sneered. "Really? Is that *really* all she wants?"

Mup lifted her sparkling hands in warning. "Mam didn't start this! She only came here because the *Speirling* stole my dad!"

Behind her, the dogs barked like crazy, fighting to get free and tackle the queen.

"Keep them *back*!" Mup yelled to Crow and Dad. "They're no match for her!"

"That's right," hissed the queen, lowering her now enormous face. "And neither is your *Mam*— with her *rebels* and her *music makers* and her filthy, contagious *combined magics*. My people will crush her like a bug."

"You leave Mam *alone*," barked Tipper, and before anyone could stop him, he squirmed free of Dad's arms and leapt to bite the queen.

"*ARGH!*" she cried, swatting him from her with a great sweep of her arm.

Tipper was flung through the air over Mup's head. With an agonized yelp, he hit the castle wall, bounced, hit the steps, and tumbled onto the hard cobbled courtyard, where he lay motionless.

"Nooo!" yelled Mup. She fired on her grandmother, lightning shooting from her palms in a great fountain of rage and horror and fear.

For a moment Mup was blinded by the column of smoke and flame that gushed from her own hands. Then her body seemed to run out of fuel. She fell abruptly to her knees. Once again, spots danced before her eyes.

Crow grabbed her by the shoulders and pulled her to her feet. She could hear him shouting through the ringing in her ears. "Run! RUN!"

Mup looked up to see her grandmother lower the hands which she had raised to protect herself from Mup's attack. The old woman seemed unharmed, though her arms were blackened to the shoulder, her white hair scorched and flecked with soot. Her eyes glittered like ice-chips in her smoke-darkened face. Behind her, the ranks of witches looked, then looked away. Obviously trusting in the strength of their queen, they went back to firing at the sky. The queen did not speak — simply rose to her enormous height again, lifted her hands, and blasted Mup and Crow.

Mup didn't know where she found the strength to move, but just before the blast hit, she flung her arms upwards, causing a bubble of bright light to flare into existence around her and Crow. The queen's power roared against it, and they were hurled backwards, surrounded but untouched, like two terrified goldfish in a bowl, tossed into a sea of green fire.

They slammed into the base of the castle wall. Mup felt all her bones jar from the impact. The air gasped from her lungs. Crow cracked his head hard against the wall and flopped limply to her side. For a moment Mup couldn't move. She was drained — broken, almost — by the amount of power she'd just used to protect herself. Across the courtyard her dad ran and snatched something colourful from the flagstones just as a huge block of stone fell from the walls above. The stone shattered, and Dad hunched as debris rained down around him.

Badger barked at him from the shelter of a doorway, as if to say, This way.

Dad spun, torn between protecting the thing in his arms and running back for Mup.

To her dismay, Mup realized the thing in Dad's arms was Tipper. Her brother was a baby once more, his colourful, snow-suited body as lifeless as a doll's. Another block plummeted from the sky. Just before it hit, Badger leapt and chomped down on Dad's flight suit, pulling Dad and Tipper out of the stone's path and into the doorway. The ground thumped with the impact. The stone filled the doorway, blocking it and the room beyond from sight.

Mup tried to rise and couldn't.

With the same grin a cat might give a broke-backed mouse, the queen advanced on her. Clumsily, Mup scrabbled for Crow, determined to protect him. Something fell from her neck with a sharp tinkling of broken glass. It was the pendant. With a great gasp of glitter and light, Aunty swirled upwards, reeling as though shoved from a calm room into the teeth of a gale.

At the sight of her sister's ghost, the looming queen came to a halt. Aunty hunched and raised her hands, like a fat, wary cat unsheathing its claws. The wind, which whipped the queen's hair and snatched at Mup's and Crow's clothes, dragged at Aunty's glittering outline, smudging it. This made the queen smile.

"Well, well," she sneered. "Aren't you a mess?"

"You don't look so good yourself, dear," said Aunty. "Your face could do with a wash."

In response to her voice, the wind lulled for a moment, the choir outside the walls paused. There came a huge clap of thunder. Lightning tore the sky. It was Aunty's turn to smile.

"That's my girl," she said as the choir resumed its terrible chorus.

The top stones of the front wall floated away as the storm began to disassemble the castle from the top down. Soon the yard would be open to the outside. Soon Mam would be here.

For the first time Mup saw uncertainty in the witches' expressions. But the queen had only to look back at them and nod reassuringly. "Hold steady," she said. Her people straightened and stood firm, once again calm and ready for whatever would come through the gap in the wall.

Mup rolled painfully to her hands and knees.

"Crow?" she gasped, shaking her friend. "Are you OK?"

"What . . . what time is it?" he croaked. "Is it time for worms?"

Mup breathed a shaky laugh and helped him sit. "I think it might be time to run, Crow."

"Yes," said Aunty, her hands still held in warning against the queen. "Time for you to run, Pearl. Your mother is not in control of this battle. Once the wall breaks, it will be rebel against enforcer, and you will not stand a chance of escaping the crossfire. Take your brother and your dad and get back across the border." She smiled over her shoulder at Mup. "You'll find the way. Just follow that little twitching nose of yours. All the world is there to guide you if you ask the right questions."

Mup helped Crow to his feet. He flopped against her and didn't seem to understand what was happening. She slung his arm over her shoulder. "Can you walk, Crow?"

"By my tall hat," he mumbled, his head lolling against her neck.

"What kind of question is that? Can I walk? I'm not a baby."

Mup had to grip him firmly about his waist as he buckled at the knees.

"What about you, Aunty?" Mup did not like how the storm was scouring away at her aunty's ghost, dispersing her as glitter and mist into the tempest. Aunty was fading. Mup had a feeling that if she went this time, she wouldn't be coming back. "I don't want you to go!"

Aunty just smiled at her. "I'm sorry I hadn't the courage to let your mam be herself as she grew up, Pearl. My life made me happy, so I thought it should make everyone happy. I had no idea your mam might want to live differently. I made her waste a lot of time—limiting herself to only half of her potential. Tell her I'm sorry, won't you? Tell her . . . tell her, I hope she finds a way to be who she's truly meant to be."

The queen sneered. "Oh, we all know who my daughter thinks she's truly meant to be—but she needn't think I'm going to let it happen, sister. Don't you remember what it was like here before I took the throne? People living by all kinds of made-up rules, based on which *clann* they were in or what *animal* they fancied being. It was *chaos*—pandemonium."

"Oh, it was *not*."

"It *was!*"

"Just because you say something is bad doesn't make it bad, sister. And just because you disapprove of something doesn't mean it shouldn't exist. We shouldn't all have to live your idea of a worthy life!"

"Worthy? What was worthy about magic wasted on trinkets and sing-songs? On people casually turning themselves into bats and rabbits and goldfish? No one knew whether they were coming or going until I took charge. Mark my words, as soon as I'm gone, it'll all fall apart again. Does my daughter honestly think she can handle that?"

"I don't know what Stella can handle," said Aunty. "Or what Stella wants."

The queen lowered her huge, bitter, and somehow magnificent face to stare Aunty in the eye. "She wants my throne," she hissed. "Everyone wants my throne. The only difference is that, unlike you, she might one day be strong enough to take it."

"She's not strong enough yet," said Aunty.

The queen smiled her terrible smile. "That's right. You kept a lid on her too long, sister. You taught her nothing about how to control her powers, and now she's nothing but chaos." She straightened. "And so, I will crush her." She turned her back, dismissing her sister's ghost and the children who cowered behind it, and stalked back to her witches, who were watching as the gap in the great castle wall grew and grew.

"Aunty," whispered Mup, eyeing the calm, ready faces of the queen's people and the great howling chaos of the storm which raged beyond the wall. "Aunty, they'll kill Mam."

But Aunty was not listening. Her eyes were closed, her arms held stiffly by her sides, her hands spread, and she was whispering. After a moment, she opened her eyes, her head cocked, clearly hearing something beyond the storm and the rage of grinding stone. She looked at the queen, who was just resuming her place amongst the ranks of cold-faced witches.

"You have underestimated the power of memory, sister," whispered Aunty. "And the power of anger." She winked back at Mup. "And of love too," she acknowledged. "Goodbye, Mup. I won't be coming back this time. Best run now. Run to the border. Don't stop until you're safe."

"Goodbye?" said Mup, struggling to keep Crow on his feet. "Won't you . . . ?"

But Aunty was already walking away through the tempest, a plump old lady in a cardigan and comfortable trousers, the storm working hard to erase her transparency from the air. She swept her arms up, calling something forth from the stones beneath her feet. "You've done wrong here, sister!" she called. "You've done wrong, and it has not been forgotten."

The queen turned to her, puzzled.

"Memory has found a voice!" cried Aunty. "Anger has found a purpose. Love has found a community. Together these things will defeat you."

The flagstones began to glitter as one by one ghosts of men and women pulled their glowing bodies from the cracks. These ghosts did not look gentle. They did not look kind. They came from deep, dark rooms underground, after years of no one speaking their names. They were anger set free at last. Rising, unstoppable, into the light, they flowed from the mouths of tunnels and doorways, stalking towards their jailers, howling for revenge.

Aunty bobbed, laughing, at the head of their tide.

"Let's see you kill them twice, sister! Let's see you defeat an army of ghosts!"

As the ghosts reached the first of the appalled witches, the wall of the castle came tumbling down. A chaos of storm cloud and battle song poured through the gap.

Mup heard Aunty yell as lightning and fire blasted from the determined witches. "Run, little hare! Run!"

She didn't need to be told a third time. She gripped Crow around his waist and dragged him, as best she could, towards the place she'd last seen her dad.

The Hare,
the Hare

"Dad?" yelled Mup. "Dad, are you guys OK in there?"

Her dad's face appeared at the slim gap where the stone hadn't quite blocked the entire doorway. "Little girl!" he said, one eye peering anxiously out. "Are you all right? I can't move this rock. Wait, let me try again . . ."

He disappeared and Mup heard a thump as he flung his body against the block. It shivered slightly, dust sifting down, but the gap didn't widen. Dad's eye appeared again. "It won't budge!" he said. "I've tried and tried. Are you hurt? Is your friend hurt?" He shifted position, trying to see Crow, who had slid to the ground as soon as Mup had let him go.

"We're OK, Dad. How's Tipper? How's Badger?"

He glanced behind him, as if to check. "The . . .
the little baby seems OK. He's very frightened, though.
The dog has run off. I . . ." Dad pressed his face to the
gap again. "What's happening out there? It sounds
like a war zone."

You don't know the half of it, thought Mup. Their position was sheltered from the gutting wind, but Mup
could see lightning flashing and gouts of fire. Ghosts
and witches and people fought each other with furious intent; boiling columns of angry storm cloud
roiled the air. "We need to get out of here, Dad."

Again her dad looked behind him. She could hear
a whimpering back there, and now a familiar crying
rose up. Dad disappeared from view for a moment. A
huge boom of thunder shook the castle. Mup pressed
her back to the wall, terrified, as the stones above
her and the ground below her shivered. Rocks and
pebbles fell like hard rain. She pulled Crow deeper
into the shelter. He allowed her to put her arms
around him, and seemed perfectly content to just sit,
gaping at the chaos.

"*By my tall hat,*" he mumbled,
"*I've never seen a storm like that.*"

Dad appeared at the gap again. Tipper was in his
arms, howling. Mup squeezed her arm between the

stones and put her dusty hand on her brother's hot and terrified face. "It's OK, Tipper. It's OK. Daddy will look after you."

But Tipper was inconsolable. Dad jiggled him up and down, all the time glancing back into the space behind him. "There's a passageway behind this room," he said. "I can feel fresh air coming from somewhere. I think that might be where the dog went. I think he might be looking for a way out for us." He pressed his face to the gap again. "But I won't leave you, little girl."

"You have to, Dad! You have to take Tipper and go. Crow and I can find our own way."

Dad shifted to see Crow. "That boy is in no shape to walk."

"Dad!" Mup grabbed her dad's sleeve and pulled him down until he was looking her in the eye. "Dad, I need you to trust me. I'll get me and Crow out of here. You need to take Tipper. You need to follow Badger. I promise I'll meet you outside the castle!"

There was another boom. The stones shook around them. Tipper howled as rocks fell and dust choked the air. "Go!" shouted Mup, shoving her dad from the gap. "Run!" And, following her own advice, she heaved Crow to his feet and ran, just as a whole section of wall roared from above and shattered into the place where they'd just been.

After a couple of yards they came to the dark mouth of a tunnel. Mup staggered into it, dragging Crow like a sack, trying to put as much distance between them and the fight as possible before he stumbled again.

"I'm sorry," he gasped. "I'm sorry." He slithered through her arms and puddled to the floor, incapable of keeping his feet. "Oh," he gasped. "Oh, why won't the world stop spinning?"

Mup crouched beside him, panting, and gazed back the way they'd come. The courtyard was a distant patch of light through which figures moved furiously, hacking at each other and wrestling, firing bolts of hurt and harm.

Mup did not want to go back out there.

She glanced into the dark tunnels ahead. *I'm the hare,* she told herself. *I find my own paths.*

Hesitantly, she put her hand to the ground. She closed her eyes and imagined a safe way out of the castle. *This way,* whispered the stones. *This way.* A path stretched out in Mup's mind: mazes of dark tunnels, shaking walls, and unsteady ceilings. She opened her eyes. Was that truly her safest option?

Crow groaned again.

"Can you turn into a raven?" she whispered.

"I can't," he gasped. "Sorry."

"Please, Crow, won't you try?"

Crow rolled to his side. "I think you should just leave me," he whispered.

"I'm not leaving you!" she cried. "Come on!" She slapped his shoulder. "Try, you stubborn bird!"

He raised himself on shaking arms. He tensed his whole body. He gasped, and became a raven.

"Yes!" yelled Mup, already scrambling to her feet. "Yes! Just hold it!" She snatched him from the ground and ran into the dark, trusting in the stones and in the messages they were sending—running as fast and as far as she could for as long as she was able. "Hold on, Crow!" she yelled. "Hold on!" Crow hung limp and heavy in her arms. His beak opened and closed as he fought to keep control. Mup yelled as the breath jogged from her. "You can do it! You can do it!"

She ran, blind except for the whispers of the stones through the soles of her feet, left now, right now, straight, straight, straight. Onwards through the pressing dark, consumed with the knowledge that this was the right way to go. This was the way out. If only they could keep running.

Crow gasped. He shuddered. He became abruptly heavy in her arms and was a boy once more.

The two of them fell to the ground.

Through her rage and disappointment, Mup heard noises coming up behind them. She dragged the groaning Crow in against the wall, pressed in beside him, and told him to shush. Almost immediately people hurried past, invisible in the darkness, jostling each other along. They were gone quickly, their footsteps and urgent whispers fading into the distance like a dream.

Mup scrambled to her hands and knees, staring after them. "Did you hear that, Crow? I think they were witches running away from the battle! The way out must be close by!"

Thrilled, Mup transformed into a hare. The tunnel immediately became visible to her. She could see the fleeing witches disappearing around a far corner. Mup bounded after them. Rounding the corner, she saw a glimmer of light coming from a sloping tunnel ahead. Fresh air tickled her whiskers.

"It is the way out, Crow! We found it!"

Overhead, a muffled boom shook the castle. Dust puffed and pebbles dribbled downwards. More footsteps came racing up the tunnel. More raggedy witches running in the dark. Mup pulled herself in tight against the wall as they sped past. One of them glanced her way, and she realized that they could see her, but they did nothing about it, only ran onwards, desperate to be gone. Mup stood on her hind legs and watched them leave. She was so close to escape!

She bounded back to Crow's side. He groaned when she shook him but did not open his eyes.

"Crow," she cried, shaking him again. "Oh, Crow, please change back into a raven. I can't carry you otherwise!"

"Leave him behind."

Startled, Mup looked up into the cold face of Crow's mother. She was limping along the corridor, her steps making no noise. She seemed perfectly capable of seeing in the dark, and she regarded Mup and Crow with no expression at all. Mup cowered against the wall, thinking she'd come to fetch them for the queen, but the witch just sneered at her and limped past.

"You're running away?" gasped Mup. "You're abandoning your queen?"

"The war is lost," said the witch, "though the queen seems yet to realize it. I've no urge to stick around and be made mincemeat of by rebels and rabble-rousers. You'd best run too. The queen still thinks she can use you as leverage against your mother. She has sent hunters after you."

"Crow can't run!"

The witch did not even glance back. "You can't save everyone. Only the very young or the very stupid think otherwise."

"Carry him for me!" cried Mup, springing after her. "We'll outrun the hunters. I'll guide you on the safest paths You know I can do it. I'm the hare. I'm the stitcher of worlds. The paths talk to me."

The witch just kept walking.

"The rebels are not going to be kind to your people after this war!" cried Mup.

Almost at the corner, the witch came to a halt and turned to glare silently down at her.

"If—if you help me now," said Mup, "my mam will help you afterwards."

"I have no guarantee of that."

"I guarantee it."

"I have done terrible things in service of the queen."

"I know that."

"*Terrible* things. Do you honestly believe you'll be permitted to absolve me of them?"

Mup stayed silent at that.

The witch bent to look her in the eye, assessing her. "You had better not be making promises you don't intend to keep," she said, and she swooped past to collect Crow from where he lay.

Mup led the way up the sloping tunnel and emerged from a small arch into a dense forest whipped by storm. As she stood up into her girl-form, the witch emerged behind her, Crow unconscious in her arms. She squinted up at the sky, the wind thrashing her hair and her layers of cloaks into a frenzy.

"I don't understand," yelled Mup, gripping her hat against the storm. "Why would the queen just leave an entrance open in the side of her castle like this? Anyone could get in!"

"Look again," said the witch.

Mup looked. All she could see was a vast expanse of blank wall stretching left and right into the trees. The door they had just exited was nowhere to be seen.

"It's invisible!"

"Besides which," said the witch, "it is only an exit. No one can go back through it without the queen's key." She shifted Crow in her arms like a not-very-heavy sack of grain, briefly scanned the wind-whipped trees, and started walking. "This way," she said.

Mup stayed where she was, sniffing the stormy air.

After a few paces, the witch looked back. "This way," she repeated.

"Hush," said Mup. "I'm concentrating."

She dropped into her hare-shape and once again sniffed. Instantly she gagged. The air was foul — filled with death and hatred and horror; filled with rage and jealousy. It was the smell of war, and it hurt. Mup squeezed her eyes tight, clenched her paws against the desire to run, and forced herself to straighten. She sniffed again, searching. The witch took an impatient step towards her. But just then, Mup found what she was looking for, a faint, lovely trace on the storm: milk and Christmas trees, butter and toast.

She took off running.

Through the trees and down a path and around a corner, just in time to see her dad swinging a punch. He had Tipper cradled in one arm and was spinning as he fought, trying to keep him out of the reach of his assailants. Badger circled, back to back with him, snarling and snapping. Four raggedy witches stood around them in a ring. They kept dodging Dad's punches and Badger's snaps, that familiar not-quite-smile on their mask-like faces. Mup could tell that the witches were just toying with them. Big as Dad was, and brave as Badger was, physical strength and courage were no match for witches.

Why are they doing this? she thought, transforming to a girl even as she ran. *Their kingdom is about to fall and they waste time tormenting a powerless man and a baby. What possible use is this to them?* But looking at their faces, Mup knew the witches were doing it because it gave them pleasure. Because they could. *They really are like cats,* she thought.

She leapt through the air, snarling. "Leave my dad alone!"

One of the witches turned. He looked more offended than alarmed at the interruption of their sport. Then he twisted his hand in the air and everything froze.

Mup, Dad, Tipper, Badger—as if caught in a bubble of time—stopped moving.

Dad was frozen mid-punch, his face scrunched in anger. Badger was half off the ground, his teeth snapping empty air. Tipper had tears frozen on his cheeks. All were perfectly still, all untouched by the roaring wind that thrashed the witches' hair and clothes.

The witches left their little circle to come and stand around Mup, looking up as she snarled down at them from mid-leap. One of them touched her outstretched hand. "This is the creature the queen sent us to find," he said. His voice was like a knife, making Mup want to wince. Still she could not move.

"Let's take her." And they reached to pluck Mup from the air.

"BEGONE!" roared a voice from the path.

A flare of green light blossomed from that direction. It swept over Mup, releasing her as it hurtled the startled witches backwards through the air. The green light freed Dad and Badger and Tipper too, and they stumbled from their frozen positions, gasping.

The witches bounced from tree trunks and smashed into bushes. They slammed to the ground and lay there moving feebly like dazed beetles.

Crow's mother stalked down from the path, her free hand still upraised and crackling with leftover power. She regarded Dad, Tipper, and Badger with distaste. "Am I to carry these too?" she asked.

"No," snapped Mup, impatiently scrambling to her feet. "Dad! Come on, follow me!"

Her dad had barely time to rise to his own feet before she was leading him away through the thrashing trees, Tipper clutched protectively in his arms, Badger galloping at his heels. Overhead, the boiling sky was seared with lightning. Thunder roared so loud that Mup ducked.

Guide me, guide me, she thought, racing through the lashing branches. *Guide me, guide me home.* She trusted the forest. She trusted it. She gave up to it the image of her little house: cosy with its yellow walls and pretty garden. Her bedroom, and Tipper's bedroom, the kitchen filled with clutter. She gave up to it the pines that bordered the river, the river that gave way to the sloping hill of airy trees, the trees that looked down on the patchwork land that was not part of her world — but was her world at the same time. *Guide me there,* she thought. *Guide me.*

Shadows were rushing through the trees above now, fighting and screaming. The battle had caught up with them. Just ahead, a figure plummeted from the sky and crashed through the treetops: man, bird, man, changing as he fell, his wings on fire. He landed in an explosion of smoke. Cats poured from the bushes and leapt on his thrashing body. Ravens dived from above. More cats came to join the fray. It was impossible to tell who was fighting whom. The blood was terrible. Entire trees burst into flame. Mup ducked her head, dodged off the path, and kept running.

She glanced back. Dad ran like a demon behind

her, crashing through bushes, his eyes staring and fixed on her. He had Tipper's face pressed to his shoulder, preventing him from looking around. At his side, Crow's mother was walking expressionlessly along. Her enormous strides kept effortless pace with the racing humans. There was fire burning behind her. Her hair and clothes were lashing shadows. Mup saw that Crow was conscious. Jogging limply in his mother's arms, he stared up at her as if in a wondrous dream. Before Mup turned away, she saw him lift his grubby hand and touch her porcelain face.

I'm running, Mam, thought Mup. *I'm running. And I have everyone with me. I have everyone safe. Come home now, Mam. Come home. We're heading for the border.*

But wherever her mam was now, or whatever she was, she gave no reply.

They broke across the border into rain and night, tumbling from the chaos of the magical forest onto the slick tarmac of a back country road. The mundane world hit them like a slap. Everything was grey: grey clouds, grey rain, grey trees, grey earth. Mup reeled with the drained-out horror of it.

No, she thought. *Oh, no. Is this what home was always like?* Then her dad gripped her shoulder, his eyes looking down into hers with warm concern. "Little girl," he said. "Are you all right?"

The colours slammed back into place: the tattered orange of his flight suit, his warm-brown skin, the silver leaves over his head, the many shades of slate and blue and green in the storm clouds above.

Mup took a deep breath of blackberry-scented air. *Not less*, she thought. *Not less. Just different.*

Tipper sobbed on Dad's shoulder. Snot-smeared and damp, his face was a little puffball of misery. "It's OK, Tipper," Mup said. "We're safe now."

"Who says you are safe?" Crow's mother emerged from the trees. "You are not *safe*. The war is still raging, can't you hear it?"

Mup stepped to the treeline and listened. Above the steady drumming of the rain, a faint noise was growing. A weird cacophony of yowls and caws, the low, growling boom of thunder.

"It's going to cross over," said Crow's mother. "You'd best get to shelter."

"Mam," whispered Crow. Still in his mother's arms, he was gazing up at her, not quite believing his eyes.

The witch's face pinched in disgust, and she allowed him to slither to the ground. He wobbled and staggered, and Mup caught him before he could fall. The witch flexed her arms and shuddered as if shrugging off some unpleasant thing.

"I did as you asked," she said to Mup. "Do not forget our bargain."

She moved into the trees, then paused at the approaching noises there. "What direction are you going in?" she asked, stepping back onto the road.

Mup closed her eyes. She listened to the tarmac hissing its strange song against her feet. "Our house is that way," she said, pointing down the road.

The witch turned in the opposite direction. "Get indoors as soon as you can," she said. "I doubt the war will spread far past the border. But who can tell what might happen around a jumbled-up little scrap of nothing like you." She walked off without a backward glance, a tall woman in the pouring rain, her black clothes gathered tight against the cold.

Crow struggled free of Mup's grip and staggered out to watch her go. He swayed as if on the deck of a ship, and Mup figured the world must still be spinning for him.

"We need to go," she said gently.

Crow nodded, but still he stood, watching his mother's figure recede in the rain.

The sounds in the woods behind them were growing louder.

Mup tugged his hand. "Now, Crow."

A raven burst angrily from the trees just ahead of them, making the two of them leap. A cat shot from nowhere, sprang improbably high, and wrestled the bird to the ground in a puff of feathers. They tumbled onto the tarmac, pecking and scratching. Suddenly the air was filled with ravens. Twigs and leaves and branches rained down at the violence of their arrival. Cats were everywhere, fighting each other, fighting the birds. The noise was awful.

"RUN!" cried Mup, and they turned as one and raced as fast as they could along the rain-soaked road as the entire world exploded in yowls and caws and chaos.

Incredibly, Mup's house was just around the bend.

"I know this place!" cried Dad.

The front door was open, golden light spilling onto the storm-tossed lawn. Mup ran, her arms up, her head ducked, the battle raging around her. Up the lawn, across the drive, into the hall, and— SLAM!—the front door was shut.

They huddled in the hall as the house rattled and the windows shook. Things thudded, dead and heavy, against the roof.

"This is my home," said Dad. He looked at Mup. "You and this baby are my family!"

"Yes," said Mup.

Crow just stared all about him, clearly out of his depth.

Still carrying Tipper, Dad began to hurry from room to room, locking windows. Badger stayed with Mup as she bolted the front door. Dad dashed from the bedroom and into the kitchen, trailing Tipper's howls behind him like a siren. Realizing what Dad was about to do, Mup ran after him. He had flung himself at the back door and was struggling with the key. Mup snatched it from him before he could turn it in the lock.

"That's Mam's door," she yelled over Tipper's howls. "She's going to come home through it."

"There's only witches out there, Mup. We can't let witches in the house!"

But Mup kept the key. "That's Mam's door," she said.

She went and sat at the kitchen table, the key clutched in her hand. Outside, the battle raged, but she wasn't afraid anymore. "It'll be OK, Dad," she said. "The storm will be over soon. Then Mam will come home."

Dad jiggled Tipper up and down, looking uncertain. Crow crept silently into sight and loitered at the threshold of the kitchen. Dad's expression softened, and he pulled out a chair at the table, inviting Crow to sit.

Crow just stared and didn't move any further into the room.

Dad smiled. "I think I need to change this baby's nappy," he said.

As Dad passed by, Crow shrank back against the door frame. Dad put a hand on his shoulder and gently squeezed. "You take your time," he whispered.

As soon as Dad left, Crow crept to Mup's side. He climbed up into the chair Dad had pulled out for him. "Your mam's not coming back," he said.

"She will," said Mup, her eyes on the back door.

"She won't. Once they've gone, they never come back."

She glanced a smile at him. "It doesn't have to be like that," she said. "You wait and see."

Mup took Crow's hand, and when Dad came back, she and Crow were sitting side by side at the kitchen table, watching the unlocked door and waiting for the storm to pass.

Home

The storm lasted all night, and then, in the morning, it just stopped.

Mup didn't notice at first. She was sitting at the kitchen table with Dad and Crow. They'd sat there all night long, listening to things thudding against the roof and walls; listening to the storm tear up the garden. Dad made tea, milky and warm and sweet like always. Mup cradled her cup and watched the door and allowed her drink to go cold. She was waiting for her mam. She was waiting for her to come home. Her whole body felt tired, from the top of her head down to the tips of her toes—a big soft pillow with no bones. Her eyes burned from watching the door.

Gradually the peacefulness of the kitchen sunk in, and Mup realized that Crow and Dad were talking.

Their voices were so soft that she hadn't noticed them until the noise of the storm had gone. Dad was explaining how aeroplanes worked. Crow was sipping his cold tea, his black eyes huge over the top of his mug. Mup didn't think he was listening to what Dad was saying—not really—but he was taking in every detail of Dad's face, scanning all the lines and contours and valleys as if getting ready to paint a picture of it, or make a map.

Stiffly, Mup straightened and looked around. Tipper was asleep in the dog-bed, with Badger curled around him like an old teddy bear. Mup vaguely recalled Dad trying to get Tipper to go to bed sometime during the night. Tipper had insisted that the dog-bed *was* his bed. Eventually, Dad had given up and laid him down beside Badger.

Mup was glad Dad had given up. Her little brother looked so peaceful.

Outside, a bird began to sing. Its voice was silver and lovely over the hum of Dad's voice. Mup looked to the window and saw that the sun had risen. The sky was full of clear, early light. She got up and went to the back door and opened it.

The garden was a paradise of sparkles, every

raindrop reflecting the sun. Everything was bright and wet and new, as if the storm had washed it clean. The trees at the end of the garden were a dark band of purple shadows. Mup strained her eyes, watching them, waiting.

Behind her, Dad began quietly putting the cups into the sink. He put on the kettle.

Crow went to crouch by the dog basket.

"Little brother," he said to Tipper. "Your father is making you a bottle."

Tipper said, "Hmm?"

Badger sighed, and stretched and yawned.

Mup went outside.

The grass was wet on her feet. The sun was cold. She shivered and watched the shadows. Gradually, the kitchen went quiet behind her. She felt Dad and Crow watching her from the door.

"Mup," said Dad softly. "Come on in. You'll get a cold."

She waited.

"Muuuup?" said Tipper's sleepy voice, and Mup figured Dad must have him in his arms.

There was a sound of quiet footsteps on the grass, and Crow put his hand gently in hers.

"Mup . . ." he began.

But Mup pointed to the trees. "Look," she cried. "*Look.*"

At first there was nothing, and she began to think she'd imagined it. But then something pale glimmered in the shadows, and a tall woman stepped into the sunshine. It was Fírinne. She looked warily around, checking for danger. Then Mam emerged from the trees. She was not at all wary, and she didn't hesitate on the threshold of the sunlight. She just strode across the grass, her eyes set on her daughter and her husband and her son, who was held in her husband's arms.

She's magnificent, thought Mup.

And she was. All the sparkle of the morning seemed to be captured and flung back out into the air by her. Even though there was no breath of wind, her long hair seemed to stir with a life of its own; and though she only wore her sensible raincoat and jeans, it felt somehow as though Mam were wearing a cloak, and that cloak were swirling behind her as she walked.

"That's my Stella," murmured Dad, and Mup didn't even have to look up at him to know he was smiling the special smile he only ever kept for Mam.

Mam dropped to one knee in front of Mup, looking into her face. "You did it," she said. "You got everyone home safe. I knew you would."

"Thanks, Mam," whispered Mup. "I knew you'd come home."

Mam clutched her shoulder, and nodded, and rose to her feet. She turned her luminous face to her husband, and her expression broke into something complicated and beautiful and in love.

Dad smiled his huge, warm, lovely smile. "So," he said. "I finally got to visit the place where you were born. It wasn't half as bad as you made it out to be."

Mam ran to him and hugged him. It quickly turned into one of those kisses of theirs, the smooshy ones that always seemed to go on forever. Mup groaned in disgust. Tipper bopped Mam and Dad furiously on their heads with his bottle. They didn't even seem to notice.

"By my tall hat," said Crow, regarding them in disbelief,

"do they always act like that?"

"You'll get used to it," sighed Mup.

"Majesty," said Fírinne, coming up behind them and coughing uncomfortably. "Majesty, we must get back."

Mam broke from her kiss, spent a moment gazing up into Dad's face, kissed Tipper on the nose, and then stood aside, holding Dad's hand. She glanced back at the trees, and Mup suddenly noticed the shadows there were filled with people. Many different kinds of folk were crowded there — even some raggedy witches standing in a little huddle, all on their own. Everyone was peering anxiously out into the sunlight, and Mup's heart contracted with fear when she realized that they were waiting for Mam to return to them.

"*Majesty,*" she thought. *Fírinne called her "Majesty."*

"Mam! You're not leaving us, are you?"

Mam looked gravely down at her. "There's still so much to do over there, Mup."

"Is the queen not beaten?" asked Crow in a panic. "Are her enforcers coming back?"

"Don't worry. The queen has fled. Her people are defeated."

"But that is only the beginning," said Fírinne. "There are others, just as bad, waiting to take her place. Now that she is gone, they are ready to swoop in and impose new tyrannies on the people of our land." She turned to Mam. "Majesty," she said. "Please tell me you will not allow that to —"

"I am not a queen, Fírinne," said Mam firmly.

Fírinne flung up her hands in frustration.

Mup clutched Mam's hand. Mam crouched down to look into her daughter's face.

"Mup," she said. "My mother was a bad person — she hurt people, she filled them with hatred and with fear. I don't want to walk away from all the damage she's left behind . . . not when there's a chance that I could help mend it. I want to go back to Witches Borough. I want to help fix what my mother did there — help people learn how to work together, and how to speak freely. Help build a world where all magics are equal, and all voices, big and small, can be heard."

Mam looked up at Dad, then back to Mup. "Will you come with me?" she asked.

"Yes," said Dad without hesitation. "Yes. Absolutely. Let's go."

Mup glanced back at her house, the warm kitchen, the hallway, the bedrooms. *I like it here*, she thought. *But it's just a place, really. It's just a building.* She looked at Tipper, at Dad, at Mam, at old, grey Badger stiffly wagging his tail. *These people are my home*, she thought.

"We must bring Badger," she said.

"Of course," said Mam.

"And Tipper gets to be a baby whenever he likes, and a puppy whenever he likes."

"Yes," said Mam.

Mup took Crow's hand. "And no one ever, ever, ever gets left behind."

Mam looked solemnly at Crow. Crow looked solemnly back.

"No one," Mam told him, "will ever get left behind."

"I like the sound of that," said Crow.

"Do you trust me, Mup?" asked Mam, rising to her feet. "Do you trust me to keep these promises?" Mam's face was all dark with the sunlight behind her, and Mup couldn't quite see her expression. It didn't matter.

"I always trust you, Mam," she said. "Let's go."

And so, Mup, hand in hand with Crow, followed by Tipper and Badger and Dad, accompanied Mam back across the lawn and under the trees, back across the border to the place Mam had been born: back to a land of colour and magic, a land of dances yet to be thought of, and songs yet to be sung.

Mup's adventure continues across the border. . . .

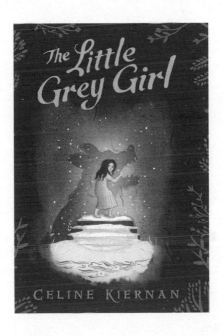

It's moving day: time for Mup, Mam and Dad, Tipper, and Crow to move into the old queen's castle. Cold and strange, the castle is haunted, both by its brutal past and its ghosts, one of whom possesses a magic that may be too much for even Mup and Mam to handle.

Turn the page for an excerpt. . . .

Over the Border to the Glittering Land

The old queen was not dead. That much was certain. No one knew where she was or how many of her witches were with her or what her plans might be— but everyone agreed that she could not be far away.

Some said she had become a storm cloud above Witches Borough, spying on everyone who spoke against her. Some said she hid behind the faces of ordinary animals, listening and watching and remembering.

Her defeat had been a trick, they said.

She was only testing them.

She would be back.

An excerpt from The Little Grey Girl

And when she returned, woe betide anyone foolish enough to have sided with her daughter.

Mam would not allow any of these rumours to stop her. In the weeks that followed the queen's defeat, she strode through all the doubts and fear with grave determination, coming and going across the border, carrying on with her plans. Finally it was time to move, and Mam came home one last time, ready to bring Mup and Dad and Tipper across the border. Ready to start their new life in the Glittering Land.

She had told Mup to bring her favourite things with her when she moved. "My mother's castle is a strange, cold place, Mup. If we are to live there, you should take some of your old life with you — to make things easier."

Mup chose her pink-and-yellow bed. She chose the writing desk and chair that Dad had made for her and that were painted with butterflies and flowers. She chose her bookcase and all her many books. She chose a mountain of multicoloured cushions and her wardrobe overflowing with rainbow-bright clothes.

That should be enough, she thought, staring at the colourful jumble piled in the frosty garden. *Enough things to fill a bedroom and make a place of my very own.*

An excerpt from The Little Grey Girl

But was it enough? Would any cushion be comfy enough to soften the cold rooms of the old queen's palace? Would any painted chair be bright enough to cancel out the darkness there?

Dad squeezed her shoulder and smiled his warm smile. "Come on, Mup. Lots to do."

He and Mup and Mam spent that whole morning staggering up and down the lawn, carrying all their things. They brought them through the dark trees at the end of their garden and down to the edge of the river, which Mup had once thought was just a stream, but which she now knew was the border to Witches Borough.

There was a raft floating there and they heaped their belongings onto it. The two steers-folk — natives of Witches Borough — leaned on their poles and eyed the growing pile as if the beds and chairs and books and blankets were the strangest things they'd ever seen.

Overhead, the branches rustled with sharp-eyed ravens. All around them the shadows flowed with watchful cats. Mup knew these were *Clann'n Cheoil* — the music people. She knew they were there to protect Mam and keep her safe. But on this side of the border the clann insisted on staying in their animal

An excerpt from The Little Grey Girl

forms, and —ashamed as she was to admit it—Mup couldn't tell one of them from the other.

You could be anyone, she thought, eyeing each cat and raven as she approached them. *You could even be a raggedy witch.*

Mup's newfound suspicion gave her friend Crow no end of grumpy amusement. But Mup wasn't willing to take any chances. Particularly when her little brother, Tipper, was still so young and her dog, Badger, was so old. Particularly when Dad hadn't a trace of magic with which to defend himself. (And as for Crow, he needed protecting too; no matter *how* loudly he protested otherwise.)

Just let someone try something, Mup thought. *Just let them try. Me and Mam will sort them out.* After everything that had happened, Mup was determined her family would never be hurt again.

At last, there was only Tipper's cot left to carry and all his baby things.

Mup helped Dad with them while Mam stood by the back door of their house, speaking with Fírinne, the leader of *Clann'n Cheoil.*

"People will never accept you as queen if you

insist on lugging your own furniture about," grumbled Fírinne.

"I've told you before," said Mam. "I am not a queen."

Fírinne tutted in impatience. "If they can't bow to you, Stella, they'll look for someone else to bow to. You need to take control. *Now*. While they're all still afraid of you."

Carrying Tipper's cot down the garden with Dad, Mup craned her neck to keep Fírinne in sight. The tall, silver-haired woman was the first friend Mup could ever remember Mam having. For all her talk of bowing, there was something fierce and proud and unbending about her. Mup liked her.

Mam gestured as if to assure her friend that she would be all right. With another tut, Fírinne stretched, transformed into a cat, and prowled grouchily off into the shadows.

Mam was left on her own, looking thoughtful.

She'll be OK, thought Mup with a twist of pride. *She's Mam. Nothing can hurt her.*

An excerpt from The Little Grey Girl

CELINE KIERNAN is the award-winning author of several novels for young people, including *Into the Grey*, which won both the Children's Books Ireland Book of the Year and Children's Choice awards, and the Moorehawke trilogy. Celine Kiernan lives in Ireland.